Kristina Beck

Maple Trees and Maybes

Maple Trees and Maybes

Copyright © 2020 Kristina Beck

ISBN: 978-3-947985-14-2

To my readers
Your excitement for my books pushes me to continue writing, no matter how hard it gets.
Thank you all for being my cheerleaders!

1

JOSH

I'm throwing in the towel. That's the last time I go out with a woman for a while. Tia and I went from heavy petting and half naked to her bolting to the bathroom to puke her brains out. Her roommate, Kelly, came home—a roommate I didn't know she had—to find me holding Tia's hair back in the bathroom. Kelly broke it to me that Tia can't hold her liquor. Wouldn't you think she'd have told me that before she had two martinis? She was barely tipsy.

Anyway, then Kelly told me that Tia lied about being a flight attendant and that she's only twenty-three, not twenty-seven. By the end of the conversation, Kelly admitted that Tia is a compulsive liar and then she, Kelly herself, fucking hit on me. I can't make this shit up. These girls are fucking whacks. What a shit show. I was out of there in seconds. I like to have a good time but not like that. Maybe I'm getting too old for this.

I open my apartment door and am surprised the

place is dark and quiet. I know it's only ten, but I can't believe Will and Lacey are asleep already. Maybe they went out. I step into the kitchen and realize the refrigerator is standing open, and then I see, illuminated in its light, Lacey. Huh? I blink and shake my head. She's naked! I gasp.

"Will, I wanted to surprise you," she protests. "Look what I—"

She turns around with a can in her hand, and I squeeze my eyes shut. She yelps and the can tumbles to the tile floor and rolls over to my feet. I look down. *Hmm.* Whipped cream.

"Josh, what the hell are you doing home?" Lacey shouts from behind the kitchen island.

I lean against the wall. Even though I'm annoyed, I can't help laughing. "You do remember that I live here, right? Or have you consumed as much alcohol as my lying, puking date did?"

"It's so early. You never come home before midnight when you have a date. Will, get out here!" she bellows.

She's right. I can't remember the last time I've come home this early. Usually, when things go well, we go back to my flavor of the day's place. I never bring women home, now that Lacey lives here.

"Will!" she yells even louder.

Where *is* he? There's faint music coming from their bedroom. Maybe he can't hear her. I grin and glance behind me. It could be fun to torture her a little.

I shrug. "Well, tonight I came back early. And now

I see why you bought whipped cream today. I thought it was to make sundaes. Do you need me to hand you the chocolate syrup or maybe caramel too? Or how about some rainbow sprinkles? They're my favorite." I toss the can up in the air and catch it.

"Josh?" Will exclaims from behind me. "Why are you home? Where's Lacey, and why's the refrigerator wide open?" He zips past me, his wet hair and shirtless body announcing where he's been.

She waves her arm in the air. "Back here. Help me!" He approaches the island, then notices Lacey crouched on the floor.

"What the hell happened? And why are you naked?" The fridge buzzer goes off, and Will closes it with his leg. The room goes dark.

I turn on the light over the kitchen table. Lacey squeals.

"Don't turn that on!"

"What? I can't see you. You're hiding behind the island." I waggle the can in my hand and look at Will. "I believe she had something exciting planned that included whipped cream."

"Will, why didn't you come out sooner? Didn't you hear me yelling for you?"

"No. I was in the shower and the music was on. I only came out to see where you were when you didn't come back."

"Whatever," Lacey whines. "Josh, can you go to your room, please? Or Will, could you get my robe? I don't particularly like being naked in the kitchen with Josh around, and I'm getting cold."

Funny, standing in front of an open fridge didn't seem to bother her.

"Aw, come on, Lace. We're roomies," I instigate, wondering why I love to annoy her so much.

Lacey snarls. I chuckle. Will shoots me a look that could kill.

"Don't be a dick." He shoves me with his shoulder, stalking past me toward the bedrooms. He quickly returns with a robe and hands it to Lacey. Seconds later, she stands up, her hands pulling the pink fabric together over her chest.

"Do you want the whipped cream back?"

She walks up to me and holds out her hand, her cheeks a fiery red. I raise it over my head instead. She pokes me in the gut and snags it when I drop my arm. Her squinty eyes bore into me.

"So what happened to your date? She didn't put out for you?" Lacey stabs, placing the can back in the fridge. "It must've been really bad if you're home by ten."

"Yeah, I can't wait to hear this." Will crosses his arms and leans against the counter, waiting with a smirk on his face.

"Where should I start?" I take a chair from the kitchen table and turn it around. Then I straddle it, leaning my arms over the back. In between their bouts of laughter, I explain what happened with my date, then smack my hands together. "I've had about as much as I can handle tonight. I'm taking a hiatus from dating."

Will coughs like he swallowed his tongue. "We'll believe that when we see it."

Lacey snorts.

"What? You don't think I can do it?"

They look at each other. "No," they say in unison.

They amaze me how in tune they are with each other. They've only been together about six months. I've never had a connection like that with a woman. Of course, I've never dated one that long either. Settling down isn't on my radar. But still.

"Is that a challenge I hear in your voices? Bring it on, people. You know I always like to win."

Will quirks a cocky eyebrow, then glances at Lacey.

"I'll handle this," she says, approaching me with an evil sneer. "I'll make it simple. You can't date, kiss, or sleep with anyone until after Drew's wedding. That's two weeks away. Think you can do it? Again, it's only two weeks. Anyone can hold off that long."

I clench my teeth because I haven't gone that long without some kind of date or sexual interaction with a woman since... I don't know when. But I love challenges, and I did say I wanted a break from women. I'll probably think differently tomorrow, but what the hell.

I inhale slowly, then exhale gustily. "Fine. Can I still flirt or talk to them?"

"Yes. But that's all. No going out for drinks, dinner... *nothing*." Lacey glances at Will. "Right, babe? Sound good? Those are easy rules to follow."

He drapes his arm over her shoulder. "I think so."

I stand up and put the chair back under the table. "What do I get if I win?"

"Five hundred bucks," Will responds immediately. "You lose, Lacey and I get five hundred."

"Are you crazy?" Lacey looks at Will like he's lost his mind.

"No, I think it's fair," I respond confidently. "The marinas are doing well. We can afford it." I reach out my hand to Will. "You've got a deal."

He shakes on it, then Lacey does too.

"Okay then. If you don't mind, I'm off to bed. I'll have to think about how I'm going to spend that well-earned cash. It looks like Christmas'll be early this year."

"Don't be so sure of yourself." Lacey chuckles. "You always want what you can't have."

"We'll just have to see about that, won't we?" I counter.

"Whatever. Get your rest. You're going to need it with the gang coming to the marina tomorrow." Her eyes brighten. "Hey, did I tell you Daisy's coming too?"

I pinch the bridge of my nose. "Yes. About a thousand times."

She thinks I have a thing for Daisy. I kind of do, but I've never admitted it. From the minute Daisy arrived at the barbecue in August in that form-fitting yellow dress, she's been haunting my dreams... Hot, steamy dreams. With that intriguing body full of tattoos, her beautiful heart-shaped face, and those striking violet-blue eyes I could drown in, her entrance commanded my attention. I've been trying to erase her from my mind ever since, but every time I hear her name or see a freakin' daisy, something weird happens inside me that I don't understand. It's like I get nervous or some shit like that. She's the *only* woman who's ever had a hold like this on me.

I turn on my heel, then stop and look over my shoulder at them. "I haven't forgotten about the whipped-cream incident a few minutes ago. Just remember, I still live here. If you want to walk around naked, maybe our living arrangements need to change. Adios."

2

DAISY

I push my windblown hair out of my face, then rub the back of my stiff neck. Ugh. Since when is this black leather armchair so uncomfortable? Or is it just me? I shift several times to find a good position.

"Daisy, you seem on edge today. More than usual," Dr. Leski speculates, writing something on her iPad with an Apple pencil. "During our last session, you were quite happy about your outlook on life."

Yeah, my professional one.

I'm not going to bother pretending that I haven't been obsessing over something or somethings. Dr. Leski has been my therapist for a year now. She's the latest in a long line of them. The previous ones were always too old and made me feel uncomfortable to talk openly. Several of them focused on my tattoos too much, as if they were the source of my problems. Far from it. They're the result of them.

Then someone recommended Dr. Leski and I said I'd go, but she was the last one I'd bother with.

Fortunately, to my benefit, we clicked. I've been seeing her ever since. Sometimes I think she knows me better than I know myself. But today, anyone would know something's up by the way I'm wiggling in this chair.

"Daisy, I hate to sound cold, but we only have forty-five minutes. I want you to get off your chest whatever's bothering you." She pauses, then asks carefully, "Did you have a relapse?"

"*Pfft*. No. God, no," I respond quickly. "Nothing like that. Don't get me wrong, the craving is always there, but I am not going to let it get out of control."

I've been a recovering alcoholic for two years. I didn't know I had a problem until my brother, Julius, caught me downing vodka straight from the bottle and following it up with a sip of orange juice for breakfast one morning. I protested until he finally got me to see that I was turning into our despicable, alcoholic, dead father. It was a major wakeup call. I sought help, and I've been dry ever since. Julius helped me get back on my feet, and my quality of life has improved every day since.

She places her tablet on the side table, then uncrosses her legs and leans forward, clasping her hands. Not her normal stance. "I'm happy and relieved to hear that," she says. "So tell me what's on your mind."

I stuff my frigid hands between my legs and rub them together. "As I've been saying, the professional side of my life is going really well. But I'm questioning the personal side. I'm sort of at a crossroads. Jules and

Sky are always together, mostly at our place. I'm starting to feel like a third wheel."

"Does it bother you that she's always there?"

"Not at all. I *love* Sky. She's the sister I never had, and she makes Jules happier than I've ever seen him. She's given us a family who's embraced us. We never thought we'd have anything like that. But I need to look further down the line. What if they get married? How would that change our living arrangements? Will he move out, or will I? Most likely me since his photography studio is connected to the penthouse. It'd be stupid for him to move out."

Her eyebrows press together. "Haven't they only been together a short while? Maybe you're worrying too much."

"Believe me, they'll get married or at least move in together. I overheard them one day. Either way, this is the push I need to be brave and get out on my own. Julius and I have relied on each other up until now, and it's all I've known. But I'm thirty-one years old. It's time to be more independent. He has Sky and… he doesn't need me like he used to."

"Have you spoken to him about it?"

I shake my head. "Not yet. I'm going to wait a while. Maybe he'll come to me."

Dr. Leski relaxes back in her chair and picks up her tablet again. "We've discussed this a bit in another session." She taps the screen a couple times. "Yes, two weeks ago you said you wanted to live a little; balance your professional life with your personal one. Maybe this is your chance to flourish."

"Maybe. I knew a day would come when Jules or I found someone." I chuckle, then whisper, "Don't tell anyone this, but I wish it would've been me."

One side of her mouth perks up. "You're still young, Daisy. You'll meet someone too."

"Maybe. But that scares the shit out of me. I'm confident when it comes to work. People think I'm a tough business chick. Well, that's what Sky and Jules say, anyway."

"You are. Never forget that," she emphasizes sincerely.

"Thanks. But what people don't know or see is that I'm this terrified girl, scarred and trapped in a thirty-one-year-old body, who thinks she'll never be worthy of any man."

How long will my abusive father have this hold over me? I hate myself for letting him win even when he's been six feet under for years. I don't think there will ever be enough sessions to convince me otherwise.

"My friends are all recovering alcoholics like me or have been abused in the past. It's a protective bubble because we all know each other's weaknesses and fears. Now I feel exposed because I'm hanging out with Sky's family and friends. Alcohol is always around."

"You don't have to spend time with them if you feel it's too tempting."

"I know. But I want to. They're a little over-whelming but a lot of fun, and I want to be a part of their family. I can't hide forever, just because alcohol might be around. I'm able to do it at Jules's openings.

I guess my concern is that they'll eventually find out about my past, and change the way they act toward me."

Dr. Leski glances at my bouncing knee. I press on it to make it stop. "I want to connect with people outside my circle. It's depressing sometimes because I feel like we only dwell on negative things."

"You don't have to tell anybody anything."

"In a way I feel like I do. What… am I only going to tell them my name and what my favorite color is?" I wonder out loud. "They're going to ask about my tattoos and why I don't drink. I don't know—maybe Sky told them already. But she doesn't know my full story. Jules said he didn't tell her everything. Only his side of the story."

"What makes you think others will block you out? You should be proud of your progress and accomplishments. There are a lot of people out there who never recover. It takes a strong person to do that. Your father was weak, so you're nothing like him. I think this is the time for you to open up and let other people in. You don't have to dump your past. Instead, let them see little pieces of you along the way as your relationships blossom."

A deep sigh escapes me. "I might be confident when it comes to my profession, but personally, I'm not sure I'll ever be."

"Let's talk about something else. I know you try to avoid this subject, but I'm curious. I've never pressed it, but today I'm going to. When's the last time you were on a date? Or let any man get close to you? Or a woman? I shouldn't assume."

"No worries. I prefer men." *I don't want to talk about my nonexistent love life.* I avert my eyes and examine the picture above her head. It's a beautiful photo of Central Park's maple trees transforming into an autumn paradise of red, orange, and yellow. It's my favorite place to run this time of year. Was that picture always there? My eyes scan the other walls, and they all have an autumn theme. No, I think they're new. They surely brighten up this room with its white walls and black leather furniture. Just like my home. White, black, and gray. I throw color accents in wherever I can.

"Daisy? When's the last time?" Dr. Leski repeats, pulling me from my internal thoughts.

"It's embarrassing to admit. Let's just say a corpse has had more dates than I've had my entire life. A dry spell is an understatement. I'm safer this way, but I'm craving a man's touch. Intimacy."

Josh's touch. He touched my lower back with his hand that day at the barbecue, and the pulse of electricity that shot through my body was enough to melt my underwear. I dream of feeling that again and hopefully much more.

"Is there anyone you're interested in? Or who's shown interest in you?"

Josh comes to mind again, and butterflies swirl in my stomach. Should I tell her?

"A smile just lit up your face." She looks at her iPad. "We're almost out of time. Tell me about him."

Her expression's full of curiosity. I know a therapist should be neutral, but I like it that she's showing emotion. It makes me even more excited for some reason.

"There is someone. Kind of. His name's Josh Hayes." I glance at the hangnail I've been playing with. Disgusting habit. I can't believe I said his name out loud. It's no longer a secret or a dream. Oh well.

"Remember our session when I cried the whole time about my dog, Chance, and I talked about a barbecue I was at when everything happened. That's where I met Josh, and I've not been able to forget him."

But maybe he's forgotten me.

She nods. "I vaguely remember a barbecue. You talked about Chance most of the time."

"Sky invited Jules and me to her brother Christian's house. We walked through the brownstone to the backyard, and the instant I walked out of that house, I noticed Josh." I can feel my smile spreading from ear to ear and I become more animated.

"He was standing off to the left, laughing with someone. It was this contagious rumble. Tall, broad, tan, gorgeous, and full of life. He had beautiful sun-streaked, light-brown hair… longer at the top and buzzed on the sides. Gray-green eyes that I could've lost myself in. His smile was brighter than the sun.

"Funny thing is, he has an identical twin brother, Will. I didn't feel anything when I was next to him, but with Josh, my body became excited just standing there, even when he wasn't talking or looking at me. It was an amazing, foreign feeling, and I've been craving it ever since. We talked a little bit, but then Jules and I had to leave unexpectedly because of Chance, and I never got to say goodbye." I stop, surprised at myself. She's the first person I've told this to.

There are a lot of other things I've never told anybody. They're locked away and... I lost that key a long time ago. Julius would have a meltdown even after all these years if he knew.

A slight grin exposes itself on Dr. Leski's face. "Have you seen him since then?"

"No." I sigh. "But I will this weekend. Drew— Sky's *other* brother—is getting married in two weeks. He and his fiancée asked a group of us to go to the Hamptons on Friday. Josh and Will own a marina there. They'll be taking us out on one of their boats."

"That sounds like fun. It's beautiful there in the fall, and the weather is supposed to be very warm this weekend. Probably the last hurrah before the cold weather blows in. Why don't you go with an open mind and with confidence? You've been through a lot, and you've come out on top. That gives you power. It's time for you to shine on your own. See how you react to him this time or how he does. Maybe you'll be disappointed, but then again, maybe you won't. This could end up being the time of your life."

"Maybe."

3

DAISY

"We're here. Time to have some fun, guys and gals," Sophia cheers. She turns to Drew and grabs his hand as the LIRR train approaches our stop. "This is the last chance for us to relax before my family arrives next weekend."

"It was a good idea to do this." He brings her hand to his lips and kisses it. I look away out of envy.

We'll be spending the day on a boat in Shinnecock Bay. I've never been there or even on a boat before. Hopefully, I won't get seasick, especially in front of Josh. My stomach turns just thinking about it.

"A weekend away is what we all need," Jocelyn says. "It's too bad Chloe had to work again. She has another big wedding she's dealing with—one of the biggest she's ever made floral arrangements for."

"I can't wait to see my wedding bouquet and everything else she's making for us." Sophia's smile is contagious. Her excitement for their wedding radiates from her entire body, not just her smile. I met Josh and Will's sister, Chloe, at the barbecue too. She was there only for a short while, though, so I didn't get to talk to her.

Jocelyn kisses her husband, Christian, on the cheek. "No computers, phone calls, meetings, dress designs or fittings, controlling of homework, temper tantrums… Nothing for forty-eight hours."

He smiles at her, but doesn't say anything. When she looks away, he glances at his phone. My impression of those two is that they're polar opposites, and he works all the time. But I've had more conversations with his sweet brother, Drew.

Jocelyn is a dress designer, and she's created Sophia's wedding dress. She also has a good friend who owns a bridal boutique. The girls ordered their bridesmaids' dresses from there, and Jocelyn's team did all the alterations. She and Sophia have kept the final design of her dress a secret. The only clue they gave was that it's a mermaid or trumpet style. For some reason, I can't picture Sophia in one like that, but what do I know?

Skylar sandwiches herself between me and Julius and says to us, "You two need this weekend more than anyone. Neither of you have left New York City in ages. Enjoy the fresh ocean air and relax."

Julius grins and gives her a squeeze. "It's not just a weekend for us. Sunday, we're off to Boston until early Tuesday morning." I gaze out the window. Why are they even bothering to go to Boston for less than two days?

I turn toward them. "Are you sure you can't stay

there longer? I can't wait to have the penthouse to myself. I don't know what I'm going to do with all the alone time." We chuckle, but I catch a peculiar glance between them. Not sure what that was about, but I don't care enough to ask.

Julius shakes his head. "Not with the shoot I have to prepare for. It's going to be hectic, both Tuesday and Wednesday."

Yippy. Some of the models who'll be there are so high maintenance.

Julius and Skylar aren't the only ones who need a break. The only alone time I get at the penthouse is when they stay at her place. That doesn't happen often, though. Julius always picks on Skylar about the mess at her small apartment. She admits she's not the tidiest person. We can see it sometimes when she stays with us. She drops her clothes and shoes at odd spots on the floor or over the furniture. I don't mind it too much because our place looks more lived in now. But if I start seeing bras and underwear, things are really going to have to change.

The train stops, and the doors slide open. We file out and hail a couple of taxis. We have reservations for Dreamy Waters Bed & Breakfast. How am I already sweating? Chilly nights and warm days, with the changing of leaves mixed in... I love it. Welcome to autumn.

They say I'm part of their circle... or *gang* is the word they use. Jocelyn, Sophia, and Lacey have welcomed me with open arms ever since Skylar started dating Julius a couple months ago. They're the nicest women I know, but sometimes I feel like the third wheel *again*—I'm the only single one. I've never been out with them like this before.

"Lacey said we should be at the marina by ten. I told you all that I called last night to make sure we could check in early," Skylar announces. "I love it that we're the only ones staying at Dreamy Waters. I can't wait to see the rooms. They looked beautiful online. Daisy, I forgot to tell you. I asked about the heated saltwater pool. You got lucky—they've kept it open because it's been so warm, but this is the last weekend for it."

"Awesome. Thanks for asking."

I can't wait to use the pool, but I really don't care what we do. I'm just excited to be out of the city. Exercise is my main go-to to counter any mental stress or cravings. When I saw the modern pool on the website, I fell in love. I don't usually swim for exercise, but this gives me something new to do. I'm tired of jogging all the time.

Julius, Skylar, and I squeeze into one taxi, and Drew and the rest pile in the other. Our taxi follows theirs to our destination. While they chat next to me, I stare out the open window, enjoying the scenery and the fresh breeze messing with my hair. The streets are lined with expensive houses and beautiful maple and oak trees, showing off their bright fall colors. I always imagined there being more dunes and sand.

Tomorrow, I plan to visit the village here. It's loaded with restaurants, boutiques, and galleries. Julius and I have been discussing the future lately. I've told him I want to expand my business—bring in more clients, and not just in photography. I studied visual arts in college. I could represent any artist. I need to not be so dependent on his work. So I've been attending a lot of art openings, looking for potential clients who don't have agents.

There's one artist I've been following closely, and he happens to be from the Southampton area. There's an opening tomorrow night at a gallery here, showing his work. That'll give me the chance to meet him in person.

The taxis pull up in front of a cream-colored colonial house with black shutters. Bright orange pumpkins and large pots of red and yellow mums line the stairs leading to the front door. A scarecrow in black-and-red flannel stands tall, guarding the house. We get out and gather our luggage. The men haul them to the front door, and we follow.

"This house is gorgeous," Sophia says. "So different from the city and from our houses in Germany."

"Lacey loves this place, and now I see why," Jocelyn gushes. "Look how perfect the front lawn is and these fall decorations. The trees, changing colors… I can just imagine how vibrant the flower beds are during the spring and summer. Roses, hydrangeas, lavender, or maybe peonies." She stops and bends over to smell a coral rose that seems to be the last one to bloom. It fits since her daughter's name is Coral. "Wow, that smells divine." Sophia bends over to smell it too.

"Oh, Daisy, look," Sky says. "There's the pool! It's calling your name." She points to the right of the house.

"Sophia, ladies… we've checked in. Come on inside," Drew calls, waving us over.

The house is cozy with different shades of blue, gray, and green accents throughout, giving it a beachy vacation atmosphere. I walk into my bedroom and wonder if someone's made a mistake—it's so huge for one person. I don't need a separate sitting area, but I'm not going to complain. I could throw a small party in my bathroom—it's double the size of the one I have at home. It even has a TV.

We take about an hour to settle in, then head out to the marina. Skylar's told me Josh and Will's marina is one of the largest in the Hamptons, but I really didn't expect there to be so many boats. Some of these yachts could easily fit thirty people at least. They're the type you see in movies. But then again, we're talking about the Hamptons. I wonder if anyone famous owns any of these. It's impressive that Will and Josh own this place. It makes Josh even more attractive because it means he's a responsible person. I linger at the back of the group with Skylar and Julius so I can look around.

"Hey, gang!" Lacey calls. She runs over with Will behind her. At least I think it's Will under the baseball cap and sunglasses. I've only met Will and Josh once and they're identical twins, so it's hard to tell. "I'm so glad you're here. Didn't we luck out with the weather. Maybe we can still go swimming."

Lacey finds Skylar and embraces her. "It's about freaking time you came to visit. You had to meet this handsome guy to finally come here." She nudges Julius then sneaks in a quick hug for him.

"Thanks for the invite, Will," Julius says. Will it is, then. Of course it is. Why would Josh follow Lacey around like that?

Lacey turns and flashes me a bright smile. "Hi, Daisy! You've changed your hair color. I love it!"

I ruffle my shoulder-length hair with my hand. "Thanks. I thought I'd go back to my natural blond. Silver blond was too much upkeep."

"Again, love it. It's so good to see you. We're going to show you a great time on the boat. Lots of sun, laughs, and bubbly."

My insides twist. I glance at Skylar and Julius. Julius tilts his head, and Skylar frowns slightly. I shake my head to tell them I'm fine. That confirms Skylar hasn't told them, or at least not Lacey, about my drinking problems. It's okay, because I told her not to. At least not yet. People always ask questions, and I really don't want to discuss it now.

Lacey wraps her arm around mine as we walk forward. "You remember Josh—Will's twin brother, right?"

"Yes. Why?" I try to act nonchalant, but my insides are flipping out.

"He's coming out with us today." She winks at me.

Huh? Did I throw off some kind of vibe that I was attracted to him at the barbecue? Maybe I'll meet him in a few minutes and wonder what the hell I was thinking. *Doubt it.*

I nod. "Oh, I know. Sky told me. I assumed he was, since he's Will's brother and they own the marina. I haven't seen him since August."

"If I remember, you both hit it off pretty well."

I don't know about that. We talked, but it was cut short. No one could have picked up on anything. *Right?* Skylar never said anything.

"Uh, quick question. How do you tell Will and Josh apart?"

She laughs. "In the beginning, it was hard. When there's time, I'll tell you a funny story about the first time I met Josh. When they're wearing sunglasses and their baseball caps, be careful. But I quickly noticed that Will has yellow specks in one of his eyes and he has a birthmark behind his left ear. It's easier now, though. Josh's hair is longer on the top, and he's a bit bulkier. Don't tell Will I said that," she mumbles.

"Thanks. Good to know."

"Be careful. Josh is quite the flirt, but that's all he's allowed to do right now."

I blink. What does that mean? He can only flirt? Is he dating someone? Is he sick? Does he have an STD?

She giggles. "You look like a deer in the headlights. Don't worry. We'll explain why later. He needs to get roasted." Oh, man. I don't even want to know what they're planning. This is the first time I've spent more than a couple of hours with them.

Maybe this wasn't such a good idea.

4

JOSH

I dodge the wasp that's been buzzing around me for the last ten minutes, and it finally flies away. It's all over the news how they're more aggressive this year, and the lingering warm weather isn't helping. Laughter catches my attention as I stand on the deck of my favorite motorboat we're going out in today. I look to the right, lean over, and brace my hands on the shiny chrome railing. The gang has arrived and are heading toward me, Will and Lacey leading the way.

When Will fell in love, he didn't just get Lacey. She came with the best group of friends anyone could ask for. They aren't just friends, they're family. And good-looking… even the guys. Every time I see them, it seems like they've brought more people under their wing. This time, it's Julius and Daisy. From what I've heard, Skylar and Julius are the real thing. Lucky me, that means Daisy will probably be around when I visit them. She'll be at the wedding too. I can't help the grin on my face.

"Hey, Josh," Skylar yells, waving her hand in the air in the back of the group. Her smile spreads from ear to ear as usual. My attention flicks to Julius, who looks like he wants to kill me, or is that his normal face? Don't worry, guy. It's not Sky I want to steal, it's Daisy. I search through the group for her beautiful face and colors. I spot her laughing with Jocelyn, and my pulse spikes. *See!* This is what I'm talking about! What is it about her? *Ignore it. The bet, remember?*

I hop off the boat onto the dock and jog over to them. "Hey, everyone!"

Drew's the first one to greet me with Sophia next to him. He extends his hand, but I shake my head. "Sorry, no can do, Drew. Ladies first." He laughs and steps to the side. I hug Sophia gently, then kiss her cheek. "Bride to be. Clock's ticking. You still have time to run off with me." I wink at her, and she slaps my arm playfully.

"Josh, is your flirt button always on?" Drew jokes.

"Hell, yes." I shake his hand. "Good to see you, man."

Jocelyn stands to the left of Sophia. "You're looking good, Josh. You never seem to lose that golden tan," she compliments me. I grab her hand and kiss the top of it.

"Hello, lovely lady. Since I'm shirtless in the sun most of the time, it isn't going anywhere."

"Hello? Her husband is right here," Christian

protests with his arms out in defeat. I drop her hand, and she snuggles up to his side. We bump fists.

"As always, the girls are lined up waiting for your attention." Skylar pokes me in the ribs.

"Today, my attention will only be on you lovely gals. Oh—and guys," I say over my shoulder, glancing at Julius and the others. Skylar snickers, and a sweet giggle comes from behind her. Daisy comes into view, and I'm happy she doesn't have her sunglasses on. Her blue eyes glisten from the rippling current slapping against the dock. My throat goes dry when her perfect pink lips curve into a smile, and I'm somehow at a loss for words.

"Josh, you remember Daisy, right? From the barbecue in August? Julius's sister." Skylar urges her forward.

Keep calm and act like you always do with any woman. "Of course. How could I forget you? You left the barbeque like Cinderella at twelve o'clock. You've changed your hair color too. Looks good." For the first time, I don't know what to do. Do I hug her? Kiss her cheek? Shake her hand?

She waits patiently in front of me, and I feel all eyes from everyone else on my back.

"What? No kiss or hug? Should I be offended or disappointed?" Daisy teases, then extends her hand to me.

I embrace it, amazed by its petal softness, then lean in and lock eyes with hers. "That's for later when no one's looking." A growl sounds behind me and a second later, Skylar pokes my side again. Daisy guffaws.

"Hands off, buddy," Skylar warns, trying not to laugh. "She's better than the riffraff you always drag home."

I stumble back. "I'm offended but then again, after my date last night, I think you're right. Just to let you know, I never bring them home." Suddenly, the women circle me. I turn around in confusion. "What did I say?"

"Date last night? Tell us more," Jocelyn inquires and crosses her arms. "We want the details. Lacey always entertains us with stories about the women you date... Mr. Bachelor."

Quickly, Lacey hip-checks Jocelyn. "Shush. You're going to get me in trouble," she mutters.

I place my hands on my hips. "Really, Lace? I don't want to know how much you've exaggerated those stories. I know how you girls like to talk when you're together." I glance around at everyone in the group. "Don't listen to a word she says. Or should I tell them what you wanted to do with the whipped cream you bought yesterday?" I threaten Lacey. All heads turn in her direction. Her lips purse. *Gotcha!*

"Don't go there, or I'll tell everyone about the deal we made last night," Lacey fires back.

"Lace! Josh! I think we've had enough of a show and they've only been here for fifteen minutes. Let's get going," Will interrupts to prevent me from embarrassing them or vice versa. Not that it's any big deal to have to stay away from women. Will walks toward the boat and everyone follows.

Suddenly, I realize I'm avoiding looking at Daisy as if I'm worried about what she thinks of me. *This never happens.* Why should I care when I hardly know her? I'm a single guy who loves women. *Wait. I forgot —I'm supposed to be on a break.*

I've never seen the water so still. We're about to enter the canal. Our friend, Sawyer, agreed to be our captain today so Will and I can relax with our friends. Still, I'm up in the cockpit next to him as we head out to Shinnecock Bay. I can enjoy the view better without anyone noticing. And no, I'm not talking about the ocean.

"Time for some bubbly to start this weekend off right. Will or Josh, where's the cooler?" Sophia asks, hopping off the bench. I'm always amazed at how clear her English is. She's German and has only been living in the United States since last December, but her English is perfect. It's impressive. Her accent and mannerisms scream *American*, even though she's not.

"Who needs sunscreen? I have a big tube if you need it," Jocelyn offers, squeezing some into her hand.

"I do," Daisy answers. "I forgot to put some on at the house."

Thank God for sunglasses. I've been watching Daisy like a hawk ever since we left the marina. No one needs to see that because I'll never live it down.

She takes the sunscreen, then grabs the bottom of her pastel blue T-shirt and pulls it over her head. My mouth goes dry again, but I want to convince myself that it's only because of the saltwater in the air. She lowers her jean shorts to the ground and places them to the side, revealing a quick view of her perfect ass. I adjust my shorts and know I should look away. But it's fucking impossible.

Her bikini is a soft canary yellow, like the dress she wore at the barbecue. I remember it because it matched the yellow center of the daisy tattoos she has. The top is a belly-free short-sleeved shirt that hangs off the shoulder with a scoop neck that dips into a V, emphasizing her tempting cleavage. A short ruffle lines it from shoulder to shoulder. The bottom has a ruffle to match the top. The suit exposes how much of her toned skin is kissed with tattoos and it's more attractive than I expected. My balls already ache, and watching her slather on the sunscreen isn't helping.

Her body is covered in never-ending, pastel-colored, twisting vines of ivy that touch every part of her... just like my hands yearn to do. Scattered among the ivy leaves are daisies, butterflies, and other random flowers. I can't see them clearly from up here, but I remember admiring them the first time I saw her. What I like about them is the delicacy of each one. The soft colors give the tattoos a femininity that I've never seen before. They wrap around her body as if they're there to protect her from something. The ivy climbs over her belly, right up to the hem of the bikini top. My thoughts go wild, wondering if the tattoos swirl around her breasts and nipples. Or did she leave that one part of her body bare? What about her ass?

"Josh!" Sawyer yells from the wheel. "What the hell are you dreaming about? I've called your name several times."

I rub the back of my neck and turn around. "Um. I thought I saw a dolphin jump out of the water. It was really quick, so I was checking if it'd happen again."

"Bullshit. Don't play with me. I've known you since we were kids. You've had your eyes on that flower since she got on the boat. What gives?"

"*Shh.*" I glance at the group, then move closer to him. "I don't know. She's different than most girls I hang out with. This is the second time we've met, and just like the first time, I feel a strong pull toward her." He grins, and I rush on. "Hey! This stays between you and me, man. Anyway, Sky says Daisy is a killer agent and awesome at her job. I can see that, but there's also this… *innocence* about her that—"

"Or maybe you're just horny and looking for your next victim."

Ouch!

I punch his arm. "Not right now. I'm on a break." His shocked expression makes me laugh.

"Hey, Josh. Want a glass of champagne?" Lacey yells up from the middle of the ladder. She wrinkles her nose at Sawyer. "Sorry, dude. You're the designated driver today."

"That's fine," he responds. "It'll be more fun to

watch all you drunk bastards making fools of yourselves."

"Touché, my friend." Lacey laughs, then climbs down the ladder. I follow.

I walk over to Sophia to retrieve my glass. Everyone lifts their drinks, and I notice that Daisy is holding up a small cup of orange juice. It's either mixed with champagne or it's plain. I remember when I met her, I offered to get her a beer or wine, but she opted for water. Maybe she doesn't drink. Why do I care? It's none of my business.

Sophia makes a little speech, thanking everyone for coming this weekend and for making her feel so welcome in the United States. This is her home now, and everyone here is her extended family. "I can't wait for the wedding!" she squeals. Tears begin to flow, and the women hug. That's my hint to go back up to the cockpit. Just as I place my foot on the first step, Lacey calls my name.

I look over my shoulder. "What's up?"

"Can I tell everyone about the bet we made last night? We're all friends here." She flashes me an annoying smirk.

I put my foot back on the deck and sit on one of the ladder steps. "Now why would you want to do that? If it's to embarrass me, it's not going to work. Besides, if you do, I get to tell them what I saw last night… and it wasn't the full moon." Her left eyebrow arches.

Skylar speaks up. "Oh, I want to hear this. You

mentioned whipped cream before and Lacey zipped her lip right away. Spill it."

"This should be good," Drew adds. "Lace always gets herself into trouble. Let's hear it."

Lacey looks to Will for support, but he just puts his hands up in the air. "Don't look at me. I was in the shower. I just found you naked in the kitchen." He chuckles, then covers his mouth. "Oops."

She swats him and says, "Whose side are you on?"

He throws up his hands. "I can't take sides—I'll get my ass kicked either way."

Laughter swirls with the ocean breeze and chatter takes over. As long as this continues, I won't have to talk. The bet isn't really a big deal, but if it entertains, I aim to please.

"Stop talking down there so we can hear about this so-called bet," Sawyer yells from above. *Gee, thanks, buddy.*

"Exactly," Christian adds, then downs his drink. That's unexpected. It's nice to see him relax for once. Jocelyn squeezes his knee playfully.

Everyone stops talking, and the only noise is the motor of the boat. Heads turn back and forth between me and Lacey. I stand up. This could be fun.

"Okay. I'll tell you about the bet and let Lacey tell you what happened in the kitchen. I'm curious how she'll spin it. Long story short, I had the worst date of my life last night. I told Will and Lace that I was going to take a break from women." Some of them guffaw, and some choke on their laughter. "Let me finish."

Silence. "Will and Lace had the same reaction, so we made a bet."

Lacey can't be quiet any longer. "He's not allowed to date, kiss, or have sex until the wedding."

"No way!" Skylar exclaims.

Am I really that bad?

"He can flirt like he always does, though," Lacey clarifies.

"What happens if he loses?" Daisy asks, surprising me. I wish I could see her eyes behind those sunglasses.

"He has to pay us five hundred dollars." Lacey's response is a bit too enthusiastic. The group laughs, and she shrugs. "It's an easy way to make some good money. Christmas isn't too far away."

"And vice versa if I win," I insert.

"Good luck there, charmer. You should go to the bank right now," Skylar jokes.

"Don't you worry." I glance at Daisy, who's biting her lower lip. "It'll be a piece of cake."

Maybe not with the way my body just reacted below the belt.

5

DAISY

F*ive hundred dollars for a stupid bet?* He must really be a lady-killer if they're so confident he'll lose. How many women has he been with? Why would I even want to be with someone like him? They're probably knocking down his door. I wouldn't blame them—he's hot as hell. Even more than the last time I saw him. I'm practically melting on the deck. The light layer of stubble on his face gives him a rugged look this time. His gorgeous eyes are a sea-foam green in the bright sunlight. I can't keep my eyes off him. I'm purposely keeping my sunglasses on so it's not obvious.

His shirt was off as soon as we left the marina. So far, I see no tattoos, just pure sculpted muscle under a delicious shade of brown-sugar skin and a sprinkle of hair on his chest. Like Lacey said, he's bulkier than Will, more muscular. He probably gives good hugs. I let my eyes wander, following his physique to the waistband of his shorts and lower. I wonder what's under there. My cheeks burn, thinking about it.

My body's just about as out of control as my mind. I've never felt this spark before, that shiver that goes up my spine every time we touch. And all we did was shake hands! *Ugh, get a grip, Daisy. The guy was on a hot-and-heavy date less than twenty-four hours ago.*

I'm pulled from my haze when Lacey says, "I was butt-naked, literally. Right in front of the fucking refrigerator, holding a can of whipped cream."

"The only light was coming from the fridge," Josh explains. "All I saw was your silhouette. Well, maybe a little bit more. And really… no offense, but… you're practically my sister-in-law. I don't want to see your privates."

I can't keep quiet. "Ha! I have to agree with Josh on that one." I turn to focus on Skylar and Julius. "I hope you two are learning from this."

Sky pokes her thumb into her chest. "What? Me? I don't live with you guys. Besides, there are naked women in his studio every other day."

Drew whistles. "We're coming over during one of your shoots."

"Over my dead body," Sophia threatens. Drew takes Sophia's face in his hands and kisses her lips. I think I'm going to puke.

"Wait—" Julius catches Sky's hand and pulls her down to his lap. "So if you did live with us, you'd walk around naked? Because if the answer is yes, you're moving in tomorrow." He tickles her and she almost falls, but he catches her in time.

"Nope, not happening. Not tomorrow anyway. Maybe one day." They kiss sweetly. Yep, I'm going to puke.

"Consider yourself warned, Daisy," Josh says. I look at him and he grins. "If you find whipped cream or chocolate sauce in your kitchen, run in the other direction. Although, if you bought them for your own entertainment, call me and I'll bring the sprinkles."

He winks at me, puts on his aviator sunglasses, and walks over to the cooler. Oh, so *enticing*.

"Thanks for the warning—um—or the offer. Wait… rainbow sprinkles or chocolate?" I let it out before I could stop myself. Laughter breaks out again.

"Rainbow." Josh licks his lips like he's hungry. I rub my hand softly down my neck, then trace my collarbone.

"Behave, Josh, or Julius will kick your ass," Skylar says.

Josh stands straight and opens a bottle of water. "According to the rules, I'm allowed to flirt, and Daisy's old enough to make her own decisions." He nods toward me. "Right, Dais? How old are you? Thirty?"

"Thirty-one." I like how he called me Dais. "Plenty old."

"No way. Not when you're in that sexy bikini." He chugs some water, turns around, and climbs up the ladder.

My eyes trail his every move as I admire the muscular definition of his entire backside. I imagine touching each ripple of muscle with my fingertips, and my body hums. I might not have as much experience as he does, but my desire for him is at a mind-boggling high.

A bead of sweat trickles down my forehead, and I wonder whether I should jump into the bay or stick my head in the cooler. Maybe I could ask Josh to cool off my hot skin with an ice cube. *Listen to me!* He has no idea what his presence or words do to me. Flirting might be his everyday thing, but I'm not used to it. I search through my bag for a container of mints.

I'm sitting there drowning in my own fantasies when a hand drapes over my shoulder. "You okay?" Skylar asks with concern.

I pop a couple of mints in my mouth. "It's not the easiest thing, being around alcohol, but it's fine. I'm having a great time enjoying the sun and daydreaming."

"Let us know if it becomes too much. And don't let Josh get to you."

Too late. Maybe I want to get to him.

The guys have anchored the boat and we're all doing what we want now. Skylar is chatting with Christian, Drew, and Julius. Lacey, Jocelyn, and Sophia are floating on donuts connected to the boat, laughing like crazy. They claim the water is still warm. I'll take their word for it. I'm staying in the boat. I'll wait for the heated, saltwater pool at the house. I just want to find a place to lie down or something to recline on.

Wow. I've been living in the city all this time and never knew so much beauty was only a couple of hours away. Shinnecock Bay is breathtaking and so easy to get to from their marina. The water is still like a lake, and the wind is more like a lazy breeze. And Will and Josh get to experience this every day.

Josh jumps off the ladder. "Dais, let me show you something. Grab your towel."

I hesitate because it's been confirmed that he's always joking around. I can't tell when he's being serious.

"Don't worry. You should know by now that I don't bite. Not yet anyway." He wiggles his eyebrows.

I slap him on the arm and chuckle. "Only after the wedding, right? I'm sure the women will be lining up for you just to take a nibble." What the hell am I saying? If anyone wants a nibble, it's me.

He bumps my arm. "Come on… Don't say that. That's not how it is." He walks to the side of the boat, grabs the railing, and steps up onto the narrow ledge. "Follow me." He holds out his hand to help me up. I place it in his, and he squeezes gently. The roughness of his skin tickles mine. My lips curl up when I see his jaw tick like Julius's does when he's battling something. Are we feeling the same thing right now? He tugs, and I step up gingerly. "Don't worry," he says. "I've gotcha. Just remember to hold onto the railing. We don't want you falling overboard."

"Would you jump in to save me if I did?" This playful tone is new, but it seems to come out naturally when I'm around him.

He twists around quickly, and I lose my balance. I reach forward with my free hand and grab onto the elastic of his trunks, pulling them down.

"Whoa there!" He grabs my hand just before I pull them far enough down that I'd finally get to see where that V is leading to. *Damn.* "You're a little devil, aren't you?" He chuckles.

"I'm so sorry. It was pure reflex." *I should jump overboard and swim to land.*

"To pull my shorts down?" He eyes me over his sunglasses.

I lift my nose in the air and shake the hair away from my burning face. "And if I'd say yes, what would you do?"

"If I didn't know better, I'd say you're teasing me right now." A cocky grin transforms his mouth.

"You make it so easy. Anyway, I think I'll go back down by Sky." I glance over my shoulder quickly and deflate. *Or not.* Skylar and Julius are practically making out.

"I don't think you should, but if you do, you have to let go first."

My eyes spring wide open as I realize I'm still holding on to his junk. I mean, his trunks. I jerk my arm back like a snake is about to bite me. *Wouldn't Dr. Leski love to analyze that simile?*

That backward move has me teetering on the edge again. My other hand has a death grip on the railing, but Josh wraps his arm around my waist and pulls me to him. My breasts mesh with his chest, and my insides quake. His scent of fresh soap and sunscreen intoxicates me.

We stand in silence, staring at each other. I wish we weren't wearing sunglasses. I want to see his eyes when he looks at me. He sweeps his hands to my hips and squeezes gently. My inner thighs constrict and goosebumps form, thankfully hidden by my tattoos.

"Are you okay now?" he asks softly.

I swallow deeply, trying to calm myself. "Better than you'd think. Thanks for the double save."

"Anytime." He straightens and lets me go. "Follow me up to the sundeck." No problem… I get to stare at your pinchable ass.

He stops next to two rectangular, cream leather cushions embedded in the deck for sunbathing. "We can hang out here for a little while if you want. Let the lovebirds do whatever they're doing."

"Sure. I was hoping there was something I could stretch out on. This is perfect. Not just this, the entire boat is beautiful. Is it new?"

"Thanks. Will and I bought it last year. I love taking it out."

I spread my beach towel over the cushion and sit down, propping myself up on my hands. He does the same. We sit in comfortable silence, looking out at the sparkling bay.

"Have you ever been here before?" The teasing tone is gone.

"No. This is my first time in the Hamptons. I don't get out of the city often."

"All work and no play, huh?"

"I guess you could put it that way. Sky told me a lot about you and Will. How you met and how you live in St. Thomas half the year and own two marinas. It's impressive. When do you go back?"

"January second," he says with a hint of either disappointment or uncertainty. I can't pinpoint it.

"St. Thomas must be so beautiful. You're lucky to be able to do what you do. Which place do you consider home?"

He takes off his sunglasses and rubs his eyes. I take mine off too since the sun is shining on our backs. "I'll always call New York City home. That's where we grew up. We have a small apartment not too far from the marina here and one in St. Thomas. It's pretty tight right now with Lacey living with us. It's taken some getting used to."

"I guess the whipped cream incident didn't help."

He shrugs. "It's okay. I love Lace, and I can pick on her because she's not going anywhere. They're glued together. But something's gotta change eventually. I don't want to live with them forever. It always worked for me and Will because we're twins and inseparable... or we were. We had no other obligations. Small apartments worked well because we travel back and forth. We don't need a lot of stuff. Now that Will is with Lacey, the dynamics have changed and will keep changing. Will they get married, have kids...? You know what I mean?"

"Perfectly. Sky's always at our place. It's sounds easier than your situation. We have a penthouse with separate bedrooms and bathrooms."

"Ooh. A penthouse in the city."

"We're extremely lucky compared to what we used to live in. Anyway, I can easily hide from Sky and Jules. Granted, no matter how big the place is, I could still find one of them naked in the kitchen. Maybe I should shock them and be the one without clothes on."

"With all those gorgeous tattoos, you wouldn't be as naked."

"Who says I'm completely covered? You haven't seen what's beneath this bikini." *Whoa! Who am I?*

He angles his head toward me while his eyes dip to my chest, then slowly climb back up. "Are you trying to tempt me?" He looks behind us as if he's looking for someone. "Or did Lacey put you up to this so I'll lose the bet? I can't tell if you're being serious or not."

"Well, if I were serious and there was no bet, what would you be thinking now?" *Damn, girl. Quit shooting off your mouth.*

"Wouldn't you like to know."

Yes!

I bump his arm with my shoulder. "Let's change the subject."

"Okay. So what are you going to do tomorrow?"

"I want to walk around the village near the B&B we're staying at. There are some art galleries I'd like to check out. I've been searching for artists who might need an agent, and one person I've been following is having an opening tomorrow night at a gallery here. I want to go and introduce myself."

"Who's the artist?"

"Zane Blue. He paints beautiful watercolors. I love his beach scenes."

"No shit. I know him."

I gasp. "No, you don't!"

He laughs. "I do. His father is my dad's best friend. We hang out from time to time. I haven't seen him lately. I could call him for you."

"That would be awesome." I clasp my hands. "Wow, I can't believe you know him. What a small world!"

"Actually, I don't have plans tomorrow night. I could go with you to the opening if you'd like. As friends. No need to make the gang think we're going on a date." He rubs his elbow against mine. "Not that I *wouldn't* go on a date with you. Well, you know what I mean. The bet and all." He's adorable when he fumbles with his words.

"No, we wouldn't want that, now would we," I say dryly.

"I don't need your brother on my ass about being near his sister either. Does he always scowl, or is it just me?"

"He's not that bad, just a little protective. He's the only family I've got. We've always been a package deal until Sky came around. I don't think he'll ever approve of anyone I date. But I can't imagine you giving a shit about that. Oh, don't take that in a negative way. You just don't seem to worry about what people say. I envy you."

"In some ways you're right. Life's too short to

worry about everyone's opinion of you. I will say, though, yes, I've gone out with a lot of women, but I've always treated them with complete respect. And despite the rumors, I haven't slept with all of them." He shrugs. "People like to assume I'm a dog. I'm not going to waste my time trying to convince them otherwise. I just haven't found that one special person who will blind me from other women. Like Lacey did with Will. Maybe I never will."

"I wish I could ignore what others think. I get tired of people who look at me like I'm trash because of my tattoos. You're not supposed to judge a book by its cover."

He looks sideways at me. "I think we're more alike than we realize, Dais."

"Maybe." *Probably not.*

We sit in silence, just soaking up the sun for a few minutes. Finally, he shifts and turns in my direction. "So, you said Julius is the only family you have. Did your parents pass away, or have you lost contact with them?"

That's a nice way to put it. I open my mouth, but he keeps talking.

"My mom died suddenly, right before Will and I were to graduate from college. I always wonder what life would be like if she were still alive. Who I'd be. I don't think I'd be on this boat." The pensive look on his face captures my heart.

"Why not?"

"Her life insurance policies enabled us to buy into the two marinas we have. My uncle owns part of the one in St. Thomas because he has a hotel connected to the marina. My dad's best friend, Joe, Zane's father, is our partner in this one. Did you know that my uncle owns the hotel where Sophia and Drew are having their wedding reception? My cousin runs it."

"No, I didn't. I've only seen that hotel from the outside—it's beautiful. I can't wait to see what it looks like inside. I hear there's an excellent view from a deck on the top floor. I'll have to check it out. I think Sophia's planning to have pictures taken up there."

We're quiet again for a moment. Noise from the girls fills the silence. They're still out on the water, splashing each other and laughing away. I wouldn't trade my spot for anything right now, even though I don't like the silence between me and Josh.

"I'm sorry to hear about your mom. It's hard living without one." From the corner of my eye, I see him nod his head. "We lost my mom when I was a teenager. My father died not too long after that."

"From a broken heart?" he asks with a hint of laughter.

"Absolutely not." I can't help the disgust that rolls off my tongue, but I won't expand on it. This isn't the conversation I want to have. Luckily, he doesn't pursue it.

"So you never said yes or no for tomorrow night? It'll keep me out of trouble, and I can look at it as a cultural experience. Something new for me. I've never been to an opening before. See, you're already a good influence."

"You just walk around and look at the paintings.

Drink some free champagne if they have it. It's fun to analyze or ask the artist about the work, but you don't have to."

"Is Sky going with you?"

"Nah. I'm on my own. Sky and Jules are meeting with the others to talk about the wedding. He's agreed to take some black-and-white photographs for them. I'm just a guest, so I don't need to be there. I'm kind of surprised to be here, really."

"I'm not in the least. Once this gang brings you into their circle, you can't get rid of them. You'll never want to either. I love them. I'm so glad Will found Lacey. She's good for him. It's amazing how fast they fell for each other. I never believed in love at first sight. They proved me wrong."

"I've said that to Sky many times—how welcoming Lacey and the girls are. Anyway, I opted out of the dinner. I'll assist Jules if he needs help, but I don't need to be part of the planning." I shrug my shoulders. "I'm only here until Sunday. I want to take advantage—"

"Of me," he blurts. We both start laughing. "Sorry. I had to do it."

I shove his arm. "You're crazy. You couldn't stop flirting if your life depended on it."

"What can I say? It's my personality."

"And it's the best. I wish I had your confidence. I'm usually pretty quiet on a personal level."

"I don't believe that." He nudges my knee. If he touches me again, I'm going to attack him... not because I'm mad, either.

"Maybe it's you. I'm comfortable around you. It's nice."

"Well, then you're stuck with me tomorrow night. Or earlier if you want me to show you around before the sun sets. I can get the afternoon off. Will owes me."

"Really? I'd love to have a tour guide. It'd be a thrill to talk to Zane too. But if you can't get the afternoon off, no worries. We can meet at the gallery. Or—"

"Nope. Lace mentioned where you're staying. I can pick you up and we can walk into town. Let's exchange numbers before you leave today."

"Great. It's a date then." I press my lips together. "Sorry, slip of the tongue."

His eyes focus on my lips, then he slowly licks his bottom one. I wonder what he'd taste like. Salty, with a hint of cinnamon? I shiver, and his pupils dilate.

Maybe I'm not the only one with steamy thoughts.

6

JOSH

We ended the night at a nearby restaurant and split up a little while ago. Of all people, Christian was drunk. Not filthy drunk, but by the way Jocelyn was acting, it was not a daily occurrence. Daisy seemed uncomfortable. I opted to go to the office for a little while so I could get my head on straight. Will almost had a heart attack because, just like Christian's drunkenness, it's rare for me to be at the marina this late at night.

I'm just not in the mood to deal with Lacey and Will tonight. I have my own bedroom, sure, but I don't always feel comfortable hanging out in the living room or... Sometimes you just want to sit on the couch with only your boxers on, you know? I lost a certain degree of freedom when she moved in. Not to mention, we only have one bathroom, and that is a disaster with all her shit in there. Will asked me beforehand if I minded if Lacey moved in. I was fine with it at first, but now I'm getting antsy.

But that's not the only reason I'm here. I don't want to hear about me and Daisy anymore. The gang found us alone in the front of the boat, supposedly sitting too close to each other. That's ridiculous, of course, but the women started whispering, Julius kept skewering me with death stares, and everyone was joking about me losing the bet. We just waved it off like it was funny and the jokes were on us, but enough is enough.

I turn my chair side to side as I stare at Daisy's number on my phone. Why do I feel so strange? Why does having her number or seeing her name make me smile? *Because something happened between us today, that's why.* But what? All I know is that the closer I got to her physically, the more I wanted to touch her. The more she spoke, the more I wanted to get to know everything about her, and I don't mean how she is in bed. Don't get me wrong, that did cross my mind, especially when she was teasing me about what's under her bikini. But this is different.

We didn't get into deep stuff other than us losing our moms and her father. That was deep, but it was a quick topic. When she responded the way she did about her father, I knew the conversation was over. Then it connected to what Sky said once about how she and Julius had a bad past. I wonder what happened to them after their parents died.

Other than the convo about that, we seem to be in similar situations with our living arrangements and our jobs. She asked about the marinas and how I like going back and forth to St. Thomas. She mentioned that she hadn't been out of the city in ages. Why is that? And why is Julius her only client? I had hoped she would've mentioned why she had so many tattoos. But nope. Nada. *Wait a sec.* Come to think of it, she kept the focus on me most of the time. She's even smarter than I thought.

I rub my hands over my face, then toss my years-old baseball cap onto the desk. Mom gave me that cap, so I won't throw it out until it literally falls apart. I don't know if I'll do it then either.

I shake the mouse to wake up the computer. I scan my email box and zone in on one particular name. *Kevin Sanders.* It's a confirmation for a meeting I'm attending in the city next week. *Maybe I can meet up with Daisy too.* Okay. That was random.

Kevin owns one of the top yacht designing and manufacturing companies in the world. We have several of his yachts and motorboats at both marinas. The boat we went out on today was from his company. I had lunch with him a couple of weeks ago. He's been talking about opening a dealership in the Hamptons and offered for me to run it. With my hands-on experience and education, plus my personality, he thinks I'd be a good fit. And it's weird, but I'm actually thinking about it.

I mean, I never thought I'd want to give up the lifestyle I have. Why would I want to go to an office job when I could be around the ocean daily? I'd have to give up living in St. Thomas six months out of the year too. But it was stupid to think that Will and I would live like bachelors our entire lives.

Once Will and Lacey get married, will they still want to move back and forth every six months? What if they have kids? And if they decide to settle somewhere, where would that leave me? Running both marinas? Or would they live in the Hamptons year-round while I handle St. Thomas? No, that's out of the question. I print copies of the documents attached to the email and extend my arm to grab them from the printer, reclining back in my chair. Maybe I should sleep here tonight. Once I gather the documents, I put them in a folder and then in my leather bag to take with me on Sunday.

Talking to Daisy today and then finding this email from Kevin confirming our meeting—it's making me wake up a bit more. I can't ignore that we've got some changes coming up. I hope nobody gets burned in the end.

A ping from my phone distracts me. I smile instantly when I see Daisy's name.

> **Daisy**: Hi, Josh! Did you find out if you could take the afternoon off?
> **Me**: I'm all yours tomorrow. What time do you want me to pick you up?
> **Daisy**: I'm going to relax and take advantage of the pool. You could come for a swim first. It's heated and the weather's supposed to be great.

I start to respond but stop when I see below her name that she's typing again.

Daisy: Never mind. You probably swim every day. A heated pool is probably no big deal to you.

Me: Seeing you in that bikini again will make it a big deal.

Daisy: Haha. Just remember… you can look, but you can't touch.

Me: Grr. Don't remind me. There's no rule against fantasizing.

Daisy: It'd be interesting to be in your head when you do that.

Me: You WILL be in my head when I'm doing it.

I chuckle out loud. I wonder if she's blushing now. But what if I'm going too far?

Daisy: OMG! My face is on fire. You should write a handbook on how to flirt. It'd be a top seller. Does 1 pm work?

Me: LOL! 1 it is. See you tomorrow.

Daisy: Don't forget your bathing suit. No skinny-dipping allowed, and I promise I won't pull it down.

Me: Then count me out. I like my birthday suit, and I don't mind you undressing me.

Daisy: LOL! Thanks for the fun day. See you tomorrow.

Me: Sleep well.

I turn off my phone and stare at it lying on my desk. She's adorable and flirty. But I still think there's a vulnerability to her, so I'll have to be careful with what I say. For the first time, I'm looking forward to seeing a woman that I'm attracted to, even though I'm not allowed to act on it.

Maybe that's the way it should be.

7

DAISY

I deflate into the cozy, slate-blue armchair in my room and drop my head back. My face hurts from smiling so much today and maybe from the amount of sun I got. Josh lights me on fire. That's the only way to describe it. Every cell of my body sizzles and tingles right now. So this is what it feels like to let go of my fear and live in the moment. Flirting is so easy with him.

Even if I never get to feel his body against mine again or ever get to taste his enticing lips, I'll still be the happiest I've ever been. It's a pity about that stupid bet, but maybe it's better. If something happened between us and it went downhill, that would screw up the gang's dynamic. If we keep it at this level, I don't really have to divulge anything about my past either. Talking about the death of my parents was enough. I want pure, innocent fun.

Keep telling yourself that.

I almost smack myself. I just happen to be on a

fun weekend away, and I'm spending it with a very hot guy. That's all this is. We're barely more than strangers. And on Sunday, I'll say goodbye and get back on the train with the others. Maybe with a new client...

How crazy is it that Josh and Will know Zane Blue? What are the odds? I'd love to snag his business on my own, but when an opportunity to get a foot in the door presents itself, I'm gonna grab it. That opportunity would be Josh Hayes.

A yawn escapes my mouth, and I suddenly realize I'm exhausted. I need to find some energy to get my ass up, so I can move to the romantic four-poster bed that's patiently waiting for me. *Too bad I'll be in it alone.* I let out a long sigh. Tomorrow's going to be busy, and I'm sure there will be a million questions at breakfast when I tell everyone that I'll be hanging out with Josh most of the day. That alone requires some sleep.

I'll be smiling while dreaming of the good things to come.

Dang, it smells good in this house. My stomach rumbles so loud, I think everyone here probably heard it. I close my door behind me and head downstairs for breakfast. Everyone else is already seated around a large table covered with plates full of scrambled eggs, bacon, pancakes, bagels, and fresh fruit.

"Gooood morning!" I place my hands on Julius's shoulders and squeeze. "How'd you guys sleep? I slept like a log in the heavenly bed I have." I look around the table and burst out laughing. Everyone is a different shade of red. "I see we all got a bit of sun yesterday."

Christian isn't here. Probably hungover. *No comment.*

"We were about to send you a message." Skylar smiles. "Come, sit down." She pats the empty seat next to her.

"It's only ten thirty. What's the big deal?"

Patti, the owner of the house, comes out of the kitchen. "Good morning, Daisy. I hope you slept well. Would you like coffee or tea?" Her warm smile could start anyone's day off right.

"Yes, I did. It was wonderful. Can I please have a big cup of coffee? Thank you." She takes the rest of my order, then zooms back to the kitchen. I pour myself a cup of what looks like freshly squeezed orange juice, then place a white fabric napkin across my lap.

"We were just talking about going into town to walk around and do a little shopping," Jocelyn says. "Are you up for that? Just the girls. Lacey has to work, so she can't go. The men are going golfing."

My orange juice almost shoots across the table. I cover my nose and mouth with my hand and mumble, "Golf? Julius?"

He shrugs. "If I suck, which I'm sure I will, I'll become designated cart driver or the caddy. At least I'll be able to say I've tried it once. Maybe I'll get lucky since Christian's hung over. It's possible that he'll spend most of the time in the cart."

Jocelyn pouts. "Be nice to him. I haven't seen him like this in a long time. It's good he loosened up a bit, but he didn't have to get drunk to do it."

Been there done that. But not anymore.

I grin at Julius. "I want to see a slo-mo of you teeing off. The ball better leave the ground."

"So do you want to?" Jocelyn asks again, then nibbles on a piece of bacon.

"Thanks for asking, but I have plans." Immediate silence as everyone gapes at me. I tap my fingers on the table. "What?"

"Nothing. We just thought you'd want to hang out with us." Jocelyn shrugs.

"You know I'd love to but I want to enjoy the pool, then Josh is coming over to show me the village." Crickets. I shake my head. "So what's the problem now?"

"You're going out with Josh?" Julius asks. Like it's the most ridiculous thing he's ever heard.

"What is with you guys? Josh and I were chatting yesterday, and I told him about the opening I want to go to tonight. Ends up his family knows the artist. How crazy is that?" I slap the table so enthusiastically that Sophia jumps. *Oops.* "He offered to go with me so he could introduce us. The artist doesn't have an agent, so I thought maybe I could entice him to work with me. Josh's connection could help me out." I can practically hear their eyes blinking with surprise. My lips purse.

"So one thing led to the other and he said he'd hang out with me at the pool and then later we'll venture into the village." My coffee arrives, and I'm thankful for the distraction. I embrace the warm cup with my hands. The steamy aroma of roasted coffee beans teases my nose. There's nothing like the first sip in the morning. Or the second, third, or fourth...

"But what about the bet?" Sophia speaks up.

This bet is so stupid.

"What about it? It's not a date. We're just friends. He's not breaking any of the stupid rules."

Patti returns with a steaming stack of pancakes. I ask for a refill of coffee.

"Josh doesn't have female *friends*." Skylar uses air quotes around the word "friends."

"I don't have a lot of guy friends either." *Or any.* "There's a first time for everything. I'm going to eat before my food gets cold."

"True," Skylar agrees. "You'll prevent him from misbehaving. That's a lot of money to lose."

"What if I'm the one who misbehaves and causes him to lose?" I smile against my coffee cup. I don't know where this boldness is coming from.

"No offense, Daisy, but you're not his type."

I stop mid-sip, put my cup down slowly, then let my eyes bore into hers. "What is *that* supposed to mean?" My irritated twang must have been obvious because her eyes bug out, then she glances at Julius for support.

"I'm sorry," she says quickly. "I didn't mean

anything bad by it. You're marriage material. And he definitely is not."

"Neither am I." *Liar!* "Did you people forget that I'm in my thirties? I can take care of myself, and I don't have to answer to any of you. You make it sound like Josh is a monster. I'm glad Will isn't here to listen to you talk about his brother like this. Josh offered to hang out with me today, and I said yes. Leave it at that." I pick up the maple syrup and drench my now cold pancakes. *Thanks, guys.* Have I mentioned how much I love maple syrup? The first piece hits my lips, and I think I've gone to heaven. This is by far the best maple syrup I've ever had. I shove another piece in my mouth and close my eyes. Who cares if they're cold.

While I munch away, they agree on when to meet back here later on today. The men excuse themselves so they can meet their scheduled tee time. Skylar walks with them to the door and kisses Julius goodbye. Jocelyn and Sophia go back upstairs to retrieve Christian.

I'm enjoying my coffee when Skylar sits back down next to me. "I'm sorry, Daisy. I didn't mean to hurt your feelings." *Sip.* "Josh is a big flirt. Julius and I don't want to see you fall for it and get your heart broken." *Sip.* "He'd be easy to fall for. He's a catch."

I put my cup down and swipe my finger over a big drop of syrup on my plate. Her words sink in as I lick the heavenly sweetness off the tip of my finger.

"You make it sound like he's this horrible woman-izer. I'm aware that he's a flirt and goes out with a lot of women. You all can't seem to stop talking about it. But he's also a nice guy and he must be responsible—he owns two marinas."

"He *is* a great guy, but sometimes he doesn't know that his flirting is inappropriate. And he likes to drink. Did you tell him?"

Patti refills my coffee, and I wait for her to leave the room. Then I turn to Sky. "Look, I'm going to be really honest with you right now."

"Okay. Shoot." She leans in closer.

"You're starting to piss me off. And Jules with his death stares." Her jaw drops. "If I were offended by Josh's flirting, I'd stay away or ignore him. Don't underestimate me. I've dealt with worse in my life. A lot worse. Worse than any of you other than Julius could imagine, so give me some credit. If Josh wants to flirt, then let him. If he wants to drink, let him. And no, I didn't tell him. I'm not going to dump my past on his lap after one day of spending time with him." Wow. That was nice to get off my chest.

"Okay. Okay," she gives in. "I'll keep my mouth shut from now on. Or I'll try to anyway. You came downstairs in such a good mood, and I've ruined it." She wraps her arms around my shoulders and squeezes. "I'm sorry."

"It's fine. You're one to speak your mind. It's admirable, but sometimes it's very annoying. But thanks for caring." I squeeze her arm.

"I love you like a sister," she says. I push my plate away. I've lost my appetite. Sky seems surprised. "Are you done already? I can wait until you finish. I don't want to leave you down here alone."

I wouldn't mind eating by myself.

"It's fine. I'm done. I'll go up with you." I drop my wrinkled napkin on the table and push my chair back. Patti comes out in time for me to ask if I can take my coffee upstairs. She says yes, then tells us there will be coffee, tea, and freshly baked cookies available at three if we want a snack. I love this place. I'll have to remember to ask her where she bought the maple syrup.

Maybe I'll have a reason to come back here in the future.

8

JOSH

"So Will tells me you took the afternoon off to spend it with Daisy." Lacey rubs her hands together gleefully while I hose off the deck of a boat. "Interesting. I can already feel the five hundred bucks in my hand."

"It's not a date. We're just hanging out. There's a big difference. Besides, I haven't had a Saturday off in a while." I explain to her about the artist and how I'm going to introduce Daisy to him.

"Wow. That's awfully nice of you." Her sarcastic tone is pissing me off, so I douse her bare legs with water. "Stop that!" She laughs and wipes down the bottom of her shorts that I hit.

"Back off, and I won't have to do it again. Don't you have someone else to bug this morning? I need to finish this so I can get out of here." I turn off the hose and toss it back onto the dock, then grab a broom to brush the excess water out of the boat.

"Nah. You're the only one I want to bug."

I roll my eyes and push the broom forward.

"I like Daisy. She's cool and I like her style. A bit shy, though," she adds.

"Not when she's with me. You're intimidating when you all get together."

She stands straight and her lower lip pops out. "We are not!"

I tap the broom on the deck. "Are too. Maybe I want to hang out with her to get a break from you," I jab, but let out a chuckle too.

She crosses her arms and taps her foot. "You're not getting rid of me unless Will dumps my ass, and you know that'll never happen."

"Especially if whipped cream's involved."

She shoots daggers from her eyes. "Let it go, Josh."

I stand the broom next to me. "Now, why would I want to do that? It's fun to see you squirm and to watch your face turn as pink as the streaks in your hair."

My phone pings, and I take it out of my cargo pants. Maybe Lacey will leave me alone now.

"Whatever. I'll get out of your hair so you can't pick on me anymore. Have a great time with Daisy. Work it for her." She waves and walks away.

"Thanks. See you some time tonight. Keep your clothes on in the kitchen just in case it's earlier than later." She stops short, then continues walking, shaking her head.

I look down at my phone, and see there's a message from Daisy. My stomach spirals with excitement. I open it up, and there's a selfie of her holding onto the ledge of a large rectangular pool, angled in a way that her bright eyes match the blue color of the water reflecting behind her. It also emphasizes her perfect breasts in that damn sexy bikini from yesterday. I was hoping she'd wear one made for an old lady today. Nope! This stupid bet is going to give me the worst set of blue balls.

> **Daisy:** It's so warm and the pool is great. It's too big for one person. It's calling your name. See you soon.

I chuckle at the phone as if we're on a video call.

> **Me:** Enticing, and I don't just mean the pool. I'm leaving in a few minutes. See you soon.

I save the picture on my phone.

"What's that smile for?" Will asks, hopping onto the boat. "Who's the lucky gal?"

"Just a political meme someone sent me." I close WhatsApp.

"Let me see." Will leans forward to look at the screen.

I shake my head, then slip the phone back into my pocket. "Deleted it already."

He angles his head to the side as if he's scrutinizing me, but he doesn't say anything.

Why am I lying? Maybe deep down inside, I don't

64

want to admit that I'm starting to look at Daisy as more than a friend. I've had a perma-smile since yesterday, and my body is aching to see her. Is it because of this stupid bet, or is our chemistry that good? I think it's the latter.

"Now that we're alone," Will says, "I wanted to apologize for what happened the other night. I know it's tight in our apartment with Lacey living with us. We really didn't expect you to be home until much later. She only wanted to surprise me when I got out of the shower."

My hand shoots up. "I don't need another replay. It's really no big deal. But I think we need to figure out how we're going to handle our living arrangements in the future. It's not going to get any better when we go back to St. Thomas."

His chin drops to his chest. "Yeah, I know. I've been talking about it with Lacey."

"Oh, really?" I'd love to hear this. "I need to leave in a few minutes, but all three of us need to talk about this. Soon."

"Let's find a time when we can chat without any distractions." He motions for me to give him the broom. I gladly hand it over. "I can finish here. Get going. Enjoy the rest of the day and behave."

"Thanks. Don't forget I'm leaving tomorrow afternoon for that meeting in the city with Kevin Sanders. I might visit Dad too. If I do, I won't come back until Tuesday or Wednesday."

"That'd be good. Dad keeps asking when he's going to see one of us. It's off season and looks like it's going to be a quiet week. We can handle it without you. Stay longer if you want—Lacey and I are taking a week off in November."

"If I didn't know you better, I'd think you're trying to get rid of me so you have the place to yourselves." I punch him in the arm. "You animal."

"Think what you want. You're always here when Lacey and I want some time off. It's our turn to do the same."

"Thanks, bro." I pat him on the shoulder. "I'm out of here."

"Have fun and say hi to Daisy and Zane. And don't forget about the bet."

He had to throw it in. I ignore him and find myself walking at a faster pace so I can get to my next destination quicker.

I pull into a parking spot on the street in front of the bed and breakfast Daisy's staying at. I've passed this house a million times and always wondered what it looked like inside. It's beautiful and well maintained. The fall decorations remind me of how Mom loved to decorate at this time of year. It was her favorite season.

I turn off the car and relax with my head back. Ever since last night, I've felt like a different person. Almost like I don't know who I am. My head keeps spinning—one minute, I'm thinking about the choices I have to make in the future. Then the next minute,

I'm thinking about the woman I'm about to enjoy my afternoon off with. Actually, I've been thinking about her since we first met in August.

Maybe this bet was a good idea. It means I have to slow down and get to know Daisy in ways other than how good we could be in bed. But why should I need a bet to make me do that? I should do it automatically. Which makes me think about all the girls I've dated in the past. This is so fucked up.

I growl out loud. Enough with the analyzing. I grab my bag from the back seat and get out. I push the car door closed and start up the path to the door. Then I glance to the right of the house and see the pool. Splashing of water, like someone just dove in, tells me Daisy is still enjoying the pool, or maybe someone else is. I change direction, round the corner, and approach the patio area. I enter quietly through the gate. Daisy is doing laps. She doesn't see me approach, so I decide to sit on a nearby sun lounger. Let's see how long it takes for her to notice me.

She turns around underwater and pushes off the wall of the pool. I watch in amazement as she swims below the surface like a mermaid. Flapping her legs, then spinning around. This is what someone looks like when they're having fun. I take off my sunglasses to get a better look.

Finally, she breaks the surface in the shallow end and stands up facing me. It's as if I'm watching her in slow motion. Water kisses her glistening skin and runs down her sexy body. I'm wishing it were my lips instead. Her bikini clings to her, showing off her pert breasts and pebbled nipples. She pushes her hands through her hair with her eyes still closed and blows the water softly from her rosy lips. I should look away, but I can't keep my eyes off the most stunning woman I've ever seen. Almost like I'm in a fairy tale.

I gaze at her face, wishing she would open her eyes so I can see her baby blues staring back at me. As if she heard my wish, she rubs the water off them, then opens her eyes. They flicker, then her lips turn up into a bright smile.

"Hi, Dais. I hope I didn't scare you." I probably looked like a perv. She giggles as she wades toward me.

"Not at all. How could I be afraid when I open my eyes and see your handsome face?"

"You're mesmerizing. You looked like a mermaid."

"Really? Just like a lot of things, I haven't been in a pool in years. I used to swim like this with my mom when I was a kid. In a lake, though."

It sounds like she's a prisoner in the city. Maybe she works nonstop and has no time for anything else. That's not living.

She rests her arms on the edge. "Are you coming in or are you afraid of mermaids?"

"Something tells me I should be very afraid of you. You're grabbing my attention more than most."

"And that's a bad thing?"

"You're going home tomorrow and that leaves me without a swimming partner." I pout playfully.

She arches an eyebrow, knowing I'm full of shit,

then splashes me. "Shut the hell up and get in the water." I jump out of the way.

"Yes, ma'am."

Maybe coming here today was the best decision I've made in a long time.

9

DAISY

I pretend the cute, or should I say suave, things he says don't affect me, but they do. I won't let him know that, though. After so many years, it's easy for me to hide behind my smile. I rest my chin on my folded arms as I hang off the edge of the pool. I keep my legs paddling slowly in the water. The view is perfect.

"You're staring."

"And? Your point would be? You were staring at me too."

He nods and tosses his shirt on the chair, then kicks off his tennis sneakers. "You got me there. You, yourself, said I can look but not touch."

That I did. I could stare at his gorgeous body all day. Too bad he already has his swim trunks on. Maybe he would have changed in front of me.

Mental facepalm. Why would he do that? Where the hell is the Daisy who just told her therapist how nervous she is in situations like this?

I push off the edge and stand up, propping my hands on my hips. "Do you work out every day? You have zero fat on your body."

"You make it sound like it's a bad thing." He grins, then suddenly runs around the pool toward the deep end and does a flip into the water. A massive splash erupts as he plunks. *Show-off.* When he resurfaces, he wipes the water from his face and pushes his hair back. He's even sexier wet. "Holy shit. This is saltwater."

"So?"

"When you think you're jumping into chlorinated water and it's not, it's kind of a shock."

I move to the deeper water and submerge myself. Every once in a while, a cool breeze blows by, making me shiver, reminding me that it's autumn.

"So did the gang give you shit for hanging out with me today? Or didn't you tell them?" Josh grabs a lone red leaf floating in the water and tosses it on the grass.

"I think they're worried I'll fall for your flirty bull-shit and go home with a broken heart. My heart's pretty guarded, so I don't think that's possible." *Are you sure?* "No one's gotten to it before; what makes you any different?"

"I'm known to be quite the charmer. I think I could melt your heart with my words." He winks at me.

"*Pfft.* Do you hear yourself? Girls really fall for your cocky attitude?" *Yes—you are. Look at how your body's on fire, even though you're in the water.*

71

"Apparently so, since your friends warned you about me."

"Okay. You need to cool off that hot head of yours." I splash him several times, including in his face. He swims toward me with his eyes closed. I quickly swim backward.

"Are you finished? Because payback's a bitch." His eyes open, and it's like looking at the devil himself.

Oh, shit. I squirm back and giggle. He pounces and starts pounding me with water. I stand and turn my back to him because I'm laughing so hard, I can't breathe. Finally he stops.

I raise my hands. "Truce, truce."

"Okay. I'll stop. You can turn around."

I push the hair out of my face and rub my eyes. "Promise? If not, I'm going to kick your ass."

He lets out a hearty laugh. "Bring it on, butterfly. Try as hard as you can to push me under the water. But you have to play fair. No kicking me in the nuts or focusing on anything in that general area."

"You're no fun, but I think I can resist *that area* of yours. It must be really sensitive if you're so worried."

"You did almost pull my shorts down yesterday."

"Ugh. Don't remind me. But that was an accident."

"So you say. Now, are you going to try or are we going to stand here all day talking about my family jewels?"

I guffaw. When I catch my breath, I say, "My stomach hurts from laughing so much. Who's going to entertain me when I'm back in the city tomorrow? It's going to suck."

"You'll have to come back then to get your dose of laughter."

I angle my head to the side. "Why should I go to you? You can visit me."

"I thought we were going to play a game." Nice way to avoid that. He beckons me forward. I circle him, contemplating my attack. I know I'll lose, but I get to hang onto his heavenly body for fun. As I get behind him, I jump on him like a monkey and pull his shoulders back, then try to push his knees forward with my feet. He's like a damn tree trunk. He doesn't move at all. I let go and stand up, trying to catch my breath. This is a better workout than running. I think I need an oxygen tank.

"Pathetic. Was that a test run? Show me what you really got." He eggs me on.

"Let me think. I need a strategy." What if I pretend I'm going to pull his trunks down again and by reflex, he dips in the water? I chuckle. I think it'll work.

"Your sweet giggles aren't a good sign." He taps his wrist. "Time's ticking, butterfly. We don't have all afternoon."

Just for that, I grip the top of his trunks with both hands and tug a little. He dips just like I expected. In one slick move, I jump up and push down on his shoulders. And he's down. *Yessss!* I let go and swim back, not knowing how he'll react.

He pushes out of the water, coughing.

"Haha. I'm the winner. Loser. Loser." I form an L with my fingers and press it against my forehead.

He shakes his head to get the water off his face. His hair stands on end. *A.D.O.R.A.B.L.E.* "That was cheating," he sputters. "That was the no-go zone."

"No way. I wasn't going to pull them down. I just wanted to make you think I would so you'd get distracted. And it worked. Ha!" I slap the water in triumph.

"You're doomed." He pounces, and I try to swim away. Before I know it, his hands are on my waist, and he twirls me around. My hands grip his hard biceps. He's propped in the water like he's sitting on a chair. By instinct, I wrap my legs around his waist and sit, just to get my bearings. Close enough to feel him against me, making my body quiver.

I look up and our eyes connect. My breath whooshes out of my lungs. His light green eyes reflect a tinge of blue from the water and they wander my face slowly, then lock with mine again. The skin crinkles between his eyebrows, making him look like he's confused. Can he read my thoughts, fears, secrets, wishes…? I almost combust when he licks his plump bottom lip. A warmth grows inside my chest and the desire to kiss him is frightening.

I lean in closer but he may not have noticed, then his mouth quirks up on one side. He pulls me closer to him, his hard-on hitting my sensitive spot, almost making me go off like a firework. What have I been missing all these years? The delicious ache there is almost unbearable. He's going to kiss me. I should stop him. But to taste his warm, salty mouth just once? *Fuck it, I'll pay the five hundred dollars.* His lips against mine would be well worth it.

"Kiss me, Josh."

He nods ever so slightly, dips his head, and I part my lips.

Maybe this is a dream.

10

JOSH

I'll admit it right now—I want to kiss her. Not because of the bet. It's because I want *her*.

I dip my head, and she parts her wet lips, inviting me again to kiss her.

She screeches, then pushes away from me, shocking the hell out of me. *What the fuck?*

"Ouch! Something just stung me." She swims to the shallow end where she can stand properly. I follow her.

"Stop a second. Let me see it. Show me where."

She lifts her left arm and points to right below her shoulder. I gently hold her arm, and she stiffens. I look closely for the stinger or mark.

"The stinger and what looks like part of an ass is still in there. It was probably a wasp. They're a big problem right now."

"They were attacking me when I first got to the pool today. Little fuckers." When she curses, it's actually cute.

I blow on it lightly, and she winces. "We have to get the stinger out. Do you have tweezers?"

"Yes. Up in my room. Let's go. It hurts like a bitch." She heads for the stairs, and I lift myself out at the edge.

"You're not allergic, are you?" I hand her a towel, and she dries off quickly, avoiding the mark. I do the same.

"I don't know. I guess we'll find out if I stop breathing or blow up like a balloon."

We stop and talk to the owner, who offers an anti-histamine. Daisy refuses it and says she'll be okay. Patti gives her an ice pack, and ten minutes later, we're in her large, beautiful room, still wrapped in our towels. Daisy's upper arm is swollen around the stinger. She's shivering from being wet and holding the ice on it. Patti reminded me of my mom, and that stung my heart like the wasp that got Daisy. Even her mannerisms were similar to Mom's. It's been years, but today it feels like yesterday when I hugged her for the last time.

Daisy leads me to the spacious, modern bathroom with marble floors, sparkling glass walk-in shower and a clawfoot bathtub. I wish I had a bathroom this big in my little apartment. She searches through her makeup bag and pulls out silver tweezers from the bottom.

"Can you remove it for me? Be gentle—it's throb-bing and burning up." I take the tweezers from her hands, and she sits on the edge of the tub, angling her side toward me.

"Sure. Its butt is pretty big, so it'll be easy to grip. That wasp had no chance to survive." She chuckles despite the pain.

I lean in and try to avoid touching her, but that's impossible. "Let me know if I hurt you." She recoils when I put a little pressure on it. "Done. Got it."

"That fast? Let me see." We both lean over the sink, our heads almost touching, and observe it in the light. "Definitely a wasp with the size of that ass."

We laugh, then I wash it down the sink.

"You have gentle hands for such a big guy," she says to my reflection in the mirror. Just like that, the atmosphere changes. Electricity sparks around us intensely, like in the pool. Her fiery eyes trace my heaving chest and then slowly move up to my face. We hold each other captive with our eyes, and I'm frozen because the more I look at her, the more beautiful she becomes. *What do I do with that?*

I shake my head, then leave the bathroom. I try to forget what happened in the pool and just now. Daisy follows me.

"So what do you want to do? Your arm is pretty swollen. Are you sure you don't want the Benadryl Patti has downstairs?"

She swats the air. "Who cares. I always act funky after I take Benadryl. I have painkillers with me, and I can pick up some ointment at a pharmacy some- where. Can we still go into town? You promised you'd show me around. No wasp is going to hold me back from that."

"If you're up for it, I'm game."

"Do you want to shower? Or what's the plan for tonight?"

"My bag's by the pool. Depending on how long we're in town, I wasn't sure if I'd have time to go home and change. I can show you what I brought with me and you can tell me what's appropriate to wear for an opening."

"So you want to spend the entire afternoon and night with me. What a privilege," she sasses, then shivers.

"Get in the shower. If you don't mind, I would like to take a quick one too."

"Sure. There's even an extra robe hanging in the closet if you want it. Go get your bag and relax in the armchair. Watch TV or use the internet. The Wi-Fi code's on the table. Whatever you want. We can discuss what we want to do after." She picks up her room key and hands it to me. "Take this so you don't get locked out while I'm in the shower."

That would probably be a good thing. I should walk out of here and never come back. She's too tempting. I have to tamp down my hormones. "I can wait downstairs if you want some privacy."

"Josh." She huffs. I like the way my name flows from her alluring mouth. "You've seen me in my bathing suit, and it's not like I'm going to be walking around naked." She points to a robe hanging on a hook. "Look how fluffy and long that thing is. You won't see anything you haven't already." *Too bad.*

I walk toward the door and open it. "Enjoy your

shower." Before she can respond, I close it behind me without looking back.

The house is silent and I'm standing in the middle of the hallway on the second floor. I shove one hand through my hair and wonder what the hell I'm doing. Am I really attracted to her, or is this just because I can't touch a woman sexually until the wedding? In a way, I wish the fucking wedding were tomorrow so I could get this bet over with and resume my normal social life. And to see if Daisy really has gotten under my skin. I think I already know the answer.

With heavy legs, I force myself down the hallway, stairs, and out the door leading to the pool. I sit on a sun lounger and put my head in my hands. I hear the screen door open and then shut. Maybe it's Daisy already. How long have I been sitting out here? I turn around and find Patti struggling to open a large table umbrella.

I jump up. "Let me help you with that."

"Oh, thank you! Josh, right? My memory is atrocious sometimes."

"Yep, that's me." She steps aside while I open it. "There you go."

"Thank you." She gasps when she glances at her watch. "It's three o'clock. It's time for some home-made cookies. I can bring some out for you to enjoy. How about a coffee or cup of tea?" *Mom?*

I'm about to decline but think twice. This is a perfect excuse to stay away from the room. It'll keep the temptation at bay, and I can think about Mom.

"Sure. But I don't have a room here. I'm just visiting Daisy."

"Don't you worry. I have plenty of cookies. Take a seat at the table and relax. So what will it be? Coffee, tea, water…?" She's good at her job. Warm and sincere. Motherly.

"Black coffee and water, please."

"Will Daisy be coming out? I sure hope her arm is okay. She's not the first to get stung here this year."

"She's taking a shower. I'm think she'll be down after that. Her arm doesn't look too good, but she claims she's fine."

"Well, the Benadryl is on the table inside just in case she changes her mind. I'll be right back."

Maybe this is the distraction I need so I won't go back upstairs.

____

11

DAISY

"Josh, you can shower now. Sorry I took so long." I walk out of the bathroom with my focus on the bracelet I'm trying to fasten. No response. "Josh?"

Once it's clasped, I look up. The room's empty. Did he leave or is he still by the pool? Maybe it was wrong for me to let him stay up here while I shower, especially after we almost kissed. I lay my hand on my forehead. "I told him to kiss me," I blurt out loud. "What was I thinking?" Apparently, he was thinking the same because he was just about to brush his lips against mine. *Damn wasp had to ruin everything.*

We were in the heat of the moment, that's all. No big deal… though it makes me sad to think it might never happen. It doesn't matter. *Just pretend it never happened.*

"I don't want to pretend." *Great!* Now I'm talking to myself. Hopefully, he doesn't feel uncomfortable and that's why he didn't come back up here. Or maybe I took too long, and he gave up waiting.

There are no messages on my phone. He must be downstairs and he has my key. I search the house for him until chatter from the patio grabs my attention. Patti's voice. Curiosity takes over. I peek out the door, and my heart melts. Josh is sitting at the large patio table, his shirt back on, munching on cookies and drinking coffee with her. Almost like he's keeping her company. She's asking questions about the marina. Pride and passion drips from his mouth when he responds. It's incredibly sweet and attractive. He might go out with every woman in town, but he has so much to offer. He's sweet, polite, handsome, dedicated, hardworking, responsible, funny... and the list goes on.

I almost don't want to interrupt them. But I can't go back to my room, because he has the darn key. I push the screen door open, and they both look in my direction. He wipes his mouth and straightens in his chair. Patti pushes her chair back and stands up.

"Hi, Daisy. We were wondering if you were going to come down. How's your arm?" I angle myself and lift up the arm of my T-shirt so they can see it. She bites on her lower lip. "Ouch. That must hurt. You need to keep ice on it. You know what will help that? Yummy cookies. I'll bring some more out here before your sweet boyfriend, Josh, eats them all."

He coughs suddenly, and I giggle under my breath. "Um. We're not together." *Not that I wouldn't want to be.*

"Really? You two look so cute together. I just assumed. Sorry about that. I need to keep my mouth shut. Anyway, coffee or tea, Daisy?"

"Coffee, please. But before you go, where do you buy your maple syrup? It was delicious this morning."

"It's from a shop in the village. I can write the name down. I'll be right back with your coffee and cookies."

She goes inside and a passing breeze smacks the door shut behind her. I turn to Josh. "You're great with people. And I could see how much you love your job by your facial expressions."

"I do love it and to socialize. Every day is different at the marina—it never gets boring. That's why I don't mind working so much. But today, I chose to spend it with you instead."

"And how's it going so far?"

"Pretty damn perfect. You'll never know how much," he murmurs.

My cheeks flush. I'm not used to being complimented like this. I narrow my eyes.

"Are you just trying to butter me up or are you being serious?"

"More than serious. A change in surroundings is just what I needed to get my head on straight. Now let me take that shower so we can finally check out the village. It's getting late."

"The room's all yours. I can drink my coffee down here." I inch over to the table to sit down.

"Would you mind coming up with me? I wanted to show you the clothes I brought. Maybe they're not good enough for an opening. I have a feeling I need to iron them too." He holds up his sport bag and, yeah, I can tell already they'll be a wrinkled mess.

"If you don't mind me being up there with you, sure," I agree happily.

"Dais, it's your room. You can do whatever you want. I'm the one imposing."

I embrace his hand. "Believe me, you're not. I'd be all alone in the village right now. I couldn't have asked for better company. So now we've got that out of the way, I'll drink my coffee upstairs and read in the cozy chair by the window. Let me tell Patti."

Moments later, we enter my room with coffee and cookies. Josh tries to sneak another one, but I hold the plate out of reach. "That's it, cookie monster. The last two are mine. I'm hungry. I didn't eat lunch."

The door closes, and he casually puts his bag near the bed. I place the coffee and cookies on the side table. There's an easiness between us like it's second nature. It's nice. No awkwardness from our almost-kiss.

I stand across from him on the other side of the bed. "So let me see this outfit."

He opens his bag and takes some clothes out. "I brought khaki trousers and this blue shirt to wear with them." I reach across the bed and take the navy-blue polo shirt.

"It's perfect. Definitely needs to be ironed. Did you throw it in the bag in a wad?"

He shrugs.

"I'll iron it for you while you're in the shower."

"You don't have to. Just drink your coffee and relax." He heads over to the closet and finds the board in there. "I've been living on my own for years. I can handle it."

"If you say so." I get comfortable on the chair and stretch my legs over the armrest, then shove the cup in my mouth to hide my smile. I said it before, and I'll say it again—today, the word to describe him is *adorable*. "Can I give you my clothes to iron? I like watching you from over here."

"Sure. Your wish is my command."

"I'm just kidding. We should get a move on if we want to walk around. Or I'll put my suit on for tonight, and then we don't have to come back here."

"Now I get to see you in a sexy suit like a professional? Are you trying to kill me?"

"I'm secretly working with Lacey so you'll lose the bet."

His head whips in my direction. "Seriously?"

I burst out laughing. "You'd think I said I was going to rob a bank with that look on your face. I'm just kidding. That would be so mean. Anyway, I wanted to say how sweet it was that I found you eating cookies with Patti outside. It makes me think you want to lose. You were charming but not in a flirty way. *Easygoing* is a good word. Something tells me you don't show everyone this side of you."

Steam shoots out of the iron when he sets it upright. "I'll be honest. She reminds me of my mom. From the way she talks and her mannerisms. It felt like I was talking to her, not Patti. As if we were catching up after all this time. It was really strange but nice. That's never happened to me before." He glances at his feet. "I miss her more than I'll ever admit."

This man has a huge heart that I don't think people see or appreciate.

"It's okay to miss your mom, Josh. You don't talk about it with your family?"

He shakes his head. "I don't like talking about it. It brings back bad memories of the day she died. The more I talk about it, the more it rips my heart open. So I don't."

"That's okay too. I carry my mom with me every day. Jules and I used to talk about her a lot, but not so much anymore. It brings back bad memories for us too. But I think different than yours."

"How so?"

It was stupid for me to say that. Time to change the subject a little bit. I stand up and walk over to him, then hold out my arm. "See the butterflies sitting on the ivy leaves all over my body? Those represent my mom."

His finger softly traces the delicate lines of one of the blue ones, sending waves of desire through my veins. I swallow hard.

"She loved butterflies. She'd get so excited when she saw one. These remind me of her happier moments. And daisies were her favorite flower, hence my name and why I have daisy tattoos too."

"They're really beautiful. Your tattoo artist is a *true* artist."

"Thanks. I've told her that many times. But I'm done with tattoos."

"I've wondered about yours, but I didn't want to pry. I have more questions, but—"

I place my fingers over his mouth. "We'll leave them for another time." I'm not going down that rabbit hole and ruin one of the best days of my life. "As you said, time's ticking. It'll be dark at the pace we're going."

He observes me for a quick second, nods, and resumes ironing. This isn't going to work.

"Y'know what? Go shower and I'll finish this. Scoot over." I push him out of the way. "The girls'll probably be back soon, and we'll be ambushed with questions. I'll get dressed out here while you're showering."

"You sure?"

"Yes. Now go!"

He chuckles and heads for the bathroom. Once the door closes, I prop my hands on the ironing board. This really is the best day. So simple for anyone else, but so special to me. And I still have the rest of the day to spend with him. I can't stop the smile on my face.

A few minutes later, our clothes are ironed and hanging on hangers. The shower's still running, so that gives me a few minutes to get dressed. For a guy, he's taking a long time. I look at the clock and it's already after four. I slip into black pants and zip the back closed. Oh no, the shower's off. I rush to get my sleeveless winter-white shirt on before he walks out, totally screwing up my hair. There's a knock on the door. *Shit.*

"Daisy, are you here?" Skylar calls through the door.

Do I ignore her? Why do I feel like we're doing something wrong when we're not? Bet or no bet, we're adults. I straighten my shirt and fluff my hair.

I unlock the door and open it halfway. He might come out of the bath—

"Hey, Daisy, do you—" Too late.

Skylar pokes her head in the door as I turn toward Josh. *Thud.* That was my jaw hitting the floor. Josh stands in the doorway of the bathroom, slick with water, steam pluming around him. His hair is wild like he towel-dried it. A white towel rests low on his hips, split on the side, showing a nice bulge in the front, making my imagination go absolutely wild. The overall scene screams sex. Why is a towel any different than swimming trunks? I don't know, but it is. *Please fall to the ground.*

"Hey, Sky. Did you have fun today?" Josh acts like it's no big deal that he's in my room dressed only in a towel.

Sky looks at him and then at me. "Yes. Sorry to interrupt whatever mischief is going on in here. I just wanted to say hi. I'm going to relax in my room for a little while."

"Boo," Julius says out of nowhere. Skylar jumps out of her skin, then he wraps his arms around her waist from behind.

"Don't scare us like that." Skylar slaps his hand. He looks up smiling, then zones in on Josh. *Here we go.*

"What is he doing in your room with just a towel on?" He sounds like he's asking me, but he's still eyeing Josh. Josh stays where he is, not giving a shit. *Good.*

"Julius, my name's Josh, remember? Dais, do you have small scissors in your industrial-sized makeup bag?"

Skylar chuckles. I do too because I find this comical for so many reasons. Julius can be intimidating, but Josh seems to just take it in stride.

"I might. Take a look if you want. Your shirt and pants are hanging in the closet."

"Thanks." He grabs the hangers with his clothes and walks back to the bathroom. Before he closes the door, he says, "Wish Daisy luck with Zane Blue... even though I don't think she'll need it." He winks at me and closes the door.

My attention goes back to them. "I'd ask you guys in, but now isn't a good time. We want to leave in a few minutes."

"Seriously, Daisy. What's going on between you two? It looks awfully cozy in there. You'd think you were dating for years," Skylar says.

"And that's when it's funny. We're not. He wanted to take a shower because we were in the pool. It's saltwater, remember?"

"All afternoon?" Julius remarks with a scowl. Just like Josh mentioned.

"Jules, I'm not in the mood to be interrogated, so

back off. I'm having a great day. Don't ruin it. I think your comments are rude and make you sound like an asshole. I don't know if it's because you can't imagine me with a guy period or because I'm hanging out with Josh. Either way, it's bullshit."

"Daisy—" Julius's voice becomes softer. Too late.

"I don't care anymore. We don't have to explain ourselves to anyone. Have fun tonight and I'll see you in the morning when we have breakfast or when we check out." I close the door. Someone knocks again, most likely Julius by the hard rap, but I keep it closed and don't respond. Bickering breaks out in the hall-way. Why can't we be alone in this house? I rest my hand on the door and take a deep breath.

The bathroom door opens. "Is the coast clear?"

"Yes. I closed the door in their faces. For the life of me, I cannot understand the problem." I turn around and freeze. "Wow, look at you! The women at this opening will be wishing you were the artist. All eyes will be on you."

"There's only one set of eyes I want," he confesses with a soft expression.

"I wonder who she is."

"I think you already know. I told you, I'm all yours today."

"Well, if you put it like that, how can I complain? I'm almost done. Just need to fix my hair and we can sneak out of here."

Maybe I will get that kiss one day.

12

JOSH

She's beyond amazing. The moment we walked into the gallery, she put on her business hat and took charge. Her face radiates confidence, making her even more beautiful. We're in her world now. I introduced her to Zane and we chatted for a while. Once she started to discuss his artwork in more depth, I left her to it. It was like listening to someone speaking a foreign language. Impressive. Now I'm walking through the gallery, holding the bags full of purchases she made today.

When we finally got out of the house, we wandered down the main street of town. Off season is nice—it's not as hectic as it is during the summer. I don't come near this area during the busy months. I noticed that she gets more excited over little things like buying a magnet for the refrigerator at home, than designer bags that cost thousands.

Usually I hate shopping, but with her it was fun. We feed off each other. She always has a quick comeback when I'm joking around with her. Our interaction is completely different and more stimulating than any of the women I've dated. Ever. It makes me wonder why I went out with them. *Sex.*

We found the store that sells the maple syrup she liked. Who would've guessed that there are so many different kinds of maple syrup? I don't care. I just want to eat it. We were able to try some, and I ended up buying a couple of bottles. Not just for her, for me too. I'll have to convince Lacey to make pancakes or waffles one day. I burn everything I cook.

"Hi, handsome." I smile at the sound of her voice and turn around. Daisy's face is glowing. I think she's ready to burst with excitement from the smile that's spread from ear to ear. "Ready to leave?"

"You're finished? How did it go?"

She juts her chin to the door. "Let's go outside first. Let me carry some of the bags."

I hold the bags out of reach. "Nope—but wait. Maybe you can for a second. I want to say goodbye to Zane."

"You're going to have to stand in line."

I look around the corner, and she's right. At least five people are waiting to talk to him. "Maybe not then. I'll send him a message tomorrow. Let's go get some fresh air."

We step out the door, and Daisy pulls me off to the side, out of people's way. She tells me to put the bags on the ground. I'm confused, but I do as she says. Seconds later, Daisy jumps in my arms and hugs me tight, smacking a big kiss on my cheek.

"Thank you so much. I was ready to burst in there."

I wrap her in my arms and enjoy her body against mine. What an unbelievable feeling, to make someone so happy without expecting something in return. She slides down my body and lets go, leaving a trail of heat behind.

"Zane asked me to meet for lunch tomorrow. Can you believe it? Of course I said yes, but my train is at ten. I'm going to have to change my ticket." She paces back and forth, biting her thumb. "I wonder if I can leave my suitcase with Patti until after lunch. I don't want to lug it around."

I step in front of her and put my hands on her shoulders. Her face contorts and she pulls back a little bit, releasing a little moan.

"Oh!" I say. "I'm sorry. I forgot about your sore arm." My hands quickly find their way to her slender waist like they belong there. Her warm hands rest lightly on my chest. "Take a deep breath."

"Doesn't matter. I like where your hands are now much better." A sly curve hits her mouth. "Not sure it's going to calm me down, though."

I don't move them because I like the glint in her eyes too much.

"Listen. I'm taking the train to the city tomorrow at four because I have a meeting on Monday. We can take that train back together if you want. You can leave your stuff at my place or the marina until you're finished."

"I don't want to bother you. You've done so much already."

"And I've enjoyed doing it, so let me keep doing it. This is important to you."

"You make it hard to say no, especially if it means I get to spend more time with you. You're so easy to be around."

"It's a bonus for me too. Now, how about we go celebrate and you tell me what Zane said? I know a nice Italian restaurant not too far from here. My treat."

"Again, you spoil me. Do you treat all your girl-friends like this?" Her eyes widen and she backpedals a bit. "Not that I'm your girlfriend. Although I can see why they're knocking down your door."

She has the worst image of me. I have to change that somehow.

"I'll never tell." I take my hands away and pick up the bags. "Is that a yes to dinner? I'm sure you're hungry because I am. Those cookies weren't enough."

"I'm starving. My stomach growled like a lion when I was talking to Zane. I hope he didn't hear it."

"Let's go," I say, guiding her in the direction of the restaurant. When we get there, they seat us in a cozy corner all by ourselves. As we get comfortable, I ask, "How about a glass of champagne or wine to celebrate?"

She sucks her lips into her mouth, which is a major turn on, but I don't think that's the purpose. I think she's nervous.

"Um." She flips through the menu to the drinks.

Her finger skims down the page. "I'll just have an iced tea since I haven't eaten." Her tone has changed to something more somber. I might be reading into this, but something's off.

"Do you mind if I have a beer?"

"Nope," she says, emphasizing the P. She keeps flipping through the menu, making no eye contact.

"Do you know what you want to eat? Want to share an appetizer?"

"Sure. Why not?" Her voice is a bit peppier, but she's still not herself. I don't get it. Maybe low blood sugar?

We discuss what we want and order. The conversation is light and a bit strained. What the hell is going on? Just as I'm about to ask, the waiter comes with our drinks.

I raise my beer, and she does the same with her iced tea. "Here's to your successful day. I hope tomorrow is even better."

"Thank you." She says it quietly, then takes a sip. I reach over and take hold of her free hand that's resting on the table, surprising her.

"What's the matter, Daisy? The brightness in your eyes is gone. Your mood has changed. Did I do something wrong?"

She shakes her head. "Nothing at all. You've done everything right today." She squeezes my hand and doesn't pull away. *That's a relief.* Then she takes a big breath. "But there's something you need to know about me and… maybe it'll change the mood for the night. Or even ruin it."

I lean over the table. "Please tell me. I promise it won't change anything. If something's bothering you, get it off your chest. We spent all day together. I'd like to get to know you under the surface." Why do I care so much about her? I've never wanted to know more about other women I've been around. I've always kept them at a distance. For some reason, I want her as close to me as possible.

"There's a reason why I don't want a glass of champagne or another alcoholic drink. Actually, the urge is there, but I can't and won't act on it."

My stomach drops. *She's an alcoholic.* Her eyes wander around us. *Don't worry. No one can hear us.*

She leans in and whispers, "I'm a recovering alcoholic and have been dry for over two years now. I'm not used to telling people."

I remain silent, trying to gather my thoughts. How do I respond to that? Congratulations for being dry? Good for you? I'm at a loss for words. Her eyes beg me to say something.

"Daisy, I don't know what to say. I don't know how to respond without sounding like an ass."

"Just respond naturally."

That I can do. "At the barbecue in August, I offered to get you a wine or a beer, and you opted for water. When we were on the boat yesterday, you didn't drink champagne, and now you ordered iced tea. Yesterday, I didn't really care because we were having fun. Not that I *don't* care…"

She sips on her iced tea. I'd love to drink my beer, but I don't think I should. Should I ask her if she wants me to return it? Is it too tempting? Again, a day of firsts.

She sets her glass on the table, then rests her chin on her propped-up hand. She looks calmer now. "I'm surprised you noticed. Sky and Jules are the only ones who know in the group. I think."

"If they've told anyone, I haven't heard anything. Anyway, after spending time with you today, somewhere along the line, you aren't just Sky's friend, you've become mine too."

She angles her head to the side, a puzzled look on her face. *She thinks I'm full of shit.*

Of course, the waiter shows up at the wrong time. I want to tell him to get lost. He puts the plate of bruschetta in the center of the table, then asks if everything is all right. We both curtly answer yes. Her attention is on me again. I stumble on.

"Yes, I know I flirt and joke around all the time. No one knows when to take me seriously. But I can be serious, and I'm speaking from my heart." I pull my head back. "Just saying that seems unreal."

Her soft laughter makes me happy.

"Keep going," she urges. "I want to hear what your heart has to say."

"*Pfft.* Lay on the pressure. You had a hard time opening up, now it's my turn to be reluctant."

"Give it a try," she encourages. "I won't run out of here."

Here goes nothing. "I want to learn everything about you. Today was so out of the ordinary for me. I had fun and didn't feel like I needed to be the cool guy.

Most of the people I'm around give me the impression that's what I have to do. It's hard to explain. Or how about this... I can be myself around you. I want you to feel that same way around me. I don't want you to hide who you are. We all have a past, we all handle things differently, and we all have stuff we struggle with every day. Some more than others."

She nods. "That's why I didn't take the Benadryl today. The type Patti had has alcohol in it. I have to watch everything I drink or even eat, every second of the day. I don't use mouthwash or wear perfume because most have alcohol in them."

"Perfume?" *Who would drink that?*

"Believe me, you don't want to know. In rehab, I was taught to get rid of everything that has alcohol in it, even if it's not for ingestion."

I shake my head. "I didn't know."

"You learn something every day."

"I've learned *a lot* today."

Maybe more than I can handle.

13

DAISY

He's still here! Why? I told him I'm a recovering alcoholic. I know it's not the plague, but some people look at me differently or take a step back. Maybe he will by the end of the night.

"Do you have any questions about it? I might not answer everything."

"I have a beer on the table. How does that make you feel? Should I return it so it's out of sight?"

That's his first question?

"I'll be honest, it's not easy because I'm not usually around a lot of people who drink alcohol in front of me. We don't keep it at our place. Seeing all the alcohol on the boat and then at the restaurant… it was very tempting to have just one glass along with everyone else.

"The little group of friends I have are also recovering. We have each other's backs. If someone's having a bad day, we can call to help us get through the craving or urge just to have that one sip, that one drink. One sip could throw away everything I've worked for. And I could be back at ground zero. I promised myself I'd never do it again. Seeing Christian drunk made my stomach turn... and that was a relief for me."

"What do you do if you are tempted to drink and the desire gets uncontrollable?"

"Other than talking to Jules or my friends, I exercise, drink a lot of coffee, chew gum, or eat strong mints excessively. I have stashes everywhere. I tried smoking, but that does nothing for me. I haven't had a really bad day in a long time that I almost couldn't control myself. And I'm so thankful that I have ways to channel my urges."

"I saw you popping some mints in your mouth today when the champagne was out. How did you realize you had a problem?"

"I started off as a social drinker to brighten my darkness, and it railroaded from there. Something happened along the way and the addiction took over, but I hid it well. Jules said stuff once or twice, but I always ignored him or got defensive, depending on my mood. Then I started to get really nasty and easily irritated. One morning, he found me drinking vodka straight from the bottle, then watched me chase it with a sip of orange juice. That's when he knew I was in trouble, and he got real serious. I'm no stranger to alcoholics, and when he pointed it out, I finally woke the hell up and realized I'd turned into one myself. It wasn't my proudest moment," I confess.

He squeezes my hand. "Daisy… your proudest moment should be the moment you stopped."

He's going to make me cry. How can this be the same Josh that everyone is afraid will take advantage of me or break my heart?

"Wow. Thank you. That's about the best thing I've ever heard. I should get a tattoo or make a T-shirt that says, *My proudest moment was when I stopped.*"

"I thought you were done with tattoos?" He eyes me suspiciously.

"This might have to be the exception. I just need to find a spot where I can put it."

"Don't make me think about your naked body again," he growls. "Finish your story."

"Okay, okay. Jules got me into a rehab. He's the main reason I'm sitting with you today. Who knows where I'd be right now otherwise. He looks like he hates you because he's afraid something will make me fall off the wagon."

"Like a broken heart."

I nod then sip my iced tea. "Or being around someone who likes to party all the time." I pull my hand away from his and rest it on my lap. Not because I think he's like that. No, it's because I have to remember, *friends* don't hold hands like we are right now. I fake a little laugh. "I have to keep reassuring them that we're just friends so they'll stop worrying."

He frowns. "Does Julius act like that with all the guys you date? I mean you're thirty-one, not eighteen."

I cackle because I have no love life. "I probably

live the opposite of you. I avoid the dating scene so I don't have to explain myself or my past. There's been no reason for him to act that way until this weekend. I tried to enjoy today, thinking I could avoid this conversation."

He shakes his head and sighs. "I'm sorry, Daisy." His voice is full of sincerity. I could kiss him on the spot.

"Please don't be. I can't stand sympathy. I'm happy it's out there." Sadly, there's more to my past, but I'm not telling him that. "I only want you to understand a little bit about who I am and what I struggle with. I felt like I was lying when I ordered an iced tea. But I have to always remind myself, I don't need alcohol to celebrate or to have fun." I shrug. "Truthfully, the craving is always there—it probably will be for the rest of my life. But avoiding relationships makes life lonely at times. Everyone needs some form of human touch. I need to find someone who'll accept me for me and all that comes with me. And gives good bear hugs, of course." I chuckle, wrapping my arms around myself.

Josh says nothing, but I know he's solely focused on me. He's still listening, so I keep going. "Like Sky and Jules. He—we—have a dark past, but she fell in love with him and she accepts *us* for who we are. Everyone deserves to be loved like that. I've just never liked someone enough to want to be accepted." *Until you.*

I take a deep breath and smooth out the brick-red tablecloth. I've said enough today, and there's a strange silence. "Why don't we eat this bruschetta before our main course—" A waiter magically arrives with our steamy pasta-filled dishes. "And here they are."

We arrange the table so everything can fit, with a mishap that almost spilled my iced tea. Josh nicely orders a bottle of water for us to share and a soda for himself. My heart melts a little bit more when he gives the waiter his full glass of beer. I don't say anything because it's not necessary. He did it for me because he cares.

I pick up my fork and swirl it in the fettuccine Alfredo. "This looks so delicious." I lift the loaded fork to my mouth and glance at Josh, who's staring at me with an expression of... admiration? "Why are you looking at me like that? Are you going to make me blush again? I'll be permanently red every time I'm near you. I won't need makeup anymore."

"Daisy." His voice sounds like a soft ocean breeze, but his eyes are serious. "Thank you for sharing that with me. I know it must've been hard. Just remember, if people don't like you or don't accept you because of this, they aren't your friends. Lacey and the gang would never do that to you. And neither would I." He couldn't have said it any better.

My eyes meld with his gorgeous ones, making my heart race and my belly swirl. A sensation I'll never get sick of... but I'll miss it after tomorrow. I respond with a simple smile.

I feel like a weight's been lifted off my chest. We're quiet for a few minutes as we fill our faces. This pasta melts in my mouth. I could inhale it because I've hardly eaten today.

Finally, he says, "So, tell me about your conversation with Zane. Let's come up with a plan to convince him you're the right agent for him. I'm good at selling things and myself." He clears his throat. "Businesswise."

I snicker and roll my eyes.

Maybe my business is the only thing I should be focusing on right now. Not the guy sitting across from me.

14

JOSH

S ky warned me that Daisy had a past, and Daisy has been very open, but something tells me there's more to it than her alcohol problems. Like her tattoos. She covered her body for a reason, not just because she likes them. I'm honored that she felt comfortable enough to tell me something so private about herself.

I didn't like it when she pulled her hand away from mine. Yes, I know I was out of line for holding it to begin with. This entire day was not a date. But that's where I'm confused because I wish I could take her home, walk her to the door, and kiss her enticing mouth goodnight, but… More than that, I want to be the one who gives her bear hugs, and that freaks me the fuck out.

I'm glad she went to the ladies' room because I needed to catch my breath.

I'm a bachelor who goes out with different

women, and I like to have a good time. What's wrong with that? Alcohol is usually involved but not excessively. I know my limits. I have fun, but I never get emotionally involved with the women I'm with. Once they start getting clingy, I walk away. No one has ever made me want to stay.

Until Daisy.

How did this happen in less than forty-eight hours? It happened to Will and Lacey. Well, less than a week for them.

She's fun, intelligent, doesn't take my shit, and gives it right back to me. I can be myself when I'm with her. Not that I can't in other situations, but I don't feel like I have to entertain. When it comes to me and Will, everyone says Will is the serious one and I'm the jokester. I take things as they come and go with the flow. When something bad happens, I deal with it and move on.

Except when it came to Mom's death. I got completely wasted at a friend's house, to the point I slept in my own puke. He almost took me to the hospital. I wanted to forget for a little while. I know this is nothing compared to Daisy's struggles, but I know what she meant... I needed something to brighten the darkness. Mom's death was the darkest moment of my life.

I don't talk about Mom to anyone. Not even Will or Chloe, most of the time. I know it's avoidance, but I miss her and I don't want to get emotional about it. It won't bring her back. What nobody knows is that I try to visit her grave every time I visit my dad. And that's another way I know that Daisy's special. Telling her that I miss Mom is one of the biggest things I've ever admitted. Maybe it's because her parents died too.

Meeting Patti today was like being sucked back in time. Mom had straight, shoulder-length brunette hair that flipped up at the bottom. Patti has a similar style but it's light brown with a dusting of gray. Granted, Mom died years ago, but she'd probably be gray by now too. And her height and weight were similar. When Patti asked me if I wanted cookies, I couldn't say no. When Mom was alive, she always had cookies waiting for us. When we were all in college, she mailed packages to each of us every week. I spoke to her the night before she died. I'm thankful every day that I had the chance to tell her how much I loved her and that she was the best mom anyone could've asked for.

A hand caresses my shoulder. "I'm back. Miss me?" Daisy says playfully then sits back down.

"Every second, my sweetest of sweethearts." I lay it on thick just to hear her laugh. She releases that adorable, quiet giggle. I want to hear it over and over. She deserves to laugh and be happy.

"You're such a goofball."

"I try. Hey, Sky just texted that they're back at the B&B, hanging out on the patio. Patti lit up the chiminea. The gang wants us to hang out with them."

She takes her phone out of her handbag and glances at it. "I have a message from Sky too."

"Do you want to go?"

She shrugs. "Sure. Why not? Hopefully, they'll lay off with the comments and questions. I'm so not in the mood."

"Well, if it gets to be too much, I'll leave, and you can go upstairs." I push my chair away from the table.

"Sounds like a plan. Did you ask for the check?"

"All done. I told you it was my treat." I stand up and gather the bags.

"Thank you." She pulls her suit jacket carefully over her swollen arm, then the other. "You treat me like a queen."

"Just like you should be." I motion for her to go ahead of me and follow her to the door.

We enjoy the chilly evening as we walk back to the house. I finish telling her a story about Lacey, and she winces.

"How embarrassing for Lacey to be sick like that in front of you, Will, and Sky. And on vacation no less."

"It didn't turn Will off—they're still together. Love is blind, they say."

"So I've heard. Now when I sit there by the fire in a few minutes, I'll be picturing Lacey throwing up on your patio in St. Thomas. Horrible."

"Don't tell her I told you. It's a sensitive subject."

She stops short as we approach the house and puts her hand on my arm. "Listen to them in the back of the house. We can hear them from the street." Daisy chuckles.

I wonder how much they've had to drink or are drinking. Will it make Daisy uncomfortable?

We walk through the front door. "Why don't you go on back. I'm going to go up and put these bags in my room and get out of this stiff suit."

"That's too bad. I like you in that outfit." *Because it makes a certain part of me stiff.*

She nudges me through the living room. "Go outside and take a break from your flattery. I'm liking it a little too much." She disappears up the stairs with giggles catching my ears.

Skylar walks in with an empty wineglass in her hand. "Josh, you're back! Where's Daisy?"

"She's upstairs changing."

"How'd everything go at the opening?"

"Good. Let Daisy tell you about it when she comes out." I don't know if I should say anything about what she told me.

"Everything okay?" Sky asks over her shoulder as she wanders to the kitchen.

"You guys seem pretty comfortable in this house. You'd think it's your own. Where's Patti?"

"She's so cool and single. You should introduce her to your dad. She's been hanging out with us and told us to take whatever we want from the kitchen. She has wine and beer if you want anything."

She opens the refrigerator and takes out a bottle of white wine. I look over my shoulder to make sure no one is around, especially Daisy.

"Daisy told me about her problems with alcohol. Did you ever think about how it might be difficult for her to be around people who are drinking?" I know I'm out of line because I've only been with her this weekend, but I can't help being defensive of her.

Skylar looks at the bottle and then at me. A mixture of emotions transforms her face. "Julius and I usually don't drink in front of her. We let it slip this weekend. She's seemed to be okay with it. She hasn't said anything."

"She shouldn't have to," I say firmly. Her eyes narrow.

"Oh, and you know what's best for her after hanging out with her for one day?"

I hear someone approaching. Conversation is over.

"Hi, Josh. Want a beer? Or maybe a glass of wine?" Patti offers, placing empty bowls in the sink. So hospitable. I will definitely recommend this place to people who are looking for somewhere to stay.

"No, thanks. I'm good and I have to drive." I stuff my hands in my pockets.

"Is Daisy with you? Will she be joining us? Do you know what she likes to drink?"

"I'm sure she only wants water now since it's so late. Me too. Thanks."

"Skylar, do you want another wine?" She lifts the bottle next to Skylar's glass. "This bottle's almost empty. I can open another one."

Skylar looks at me, the wine bottle, and then at Patti.

"No, thanks. I've changed my mind. It's getting

late and we have an early morning. Water is good for me too."

"Then you two go back out and enjoy the fire. I'll bring a couple bottles of water and glasses. Josh, there are two empty chairs outside for you and Daisy."

We walk outside in silence. Everyone greets me and asks where Daisy is. I don't have to answer because she walks out the door in black leggings and an oversized gray hooded sweatshirt. She sits in one of the chairs and I take the one next to her, admiring her as the flames from the fire brighten her face.

"It's chilly tonight." Daisy rubs her hands together. "This is so nice and cozy."

Patti comes out and sets the water and glasses on the table behind Julius. She pours glasses and hands them out to whoever wants one. I take mine and place it on the ground near my chair. When I observe the gang sitting around the fire, I realize how much I like it and how it feels like home. I'd rather be here than at a bar or on a date somewhere. Because of Daisy.

I turn my attention back to her. I don't think I've ever looked at another woman the way I'm admiring her. Like she's the strongest woman I know and she radiates beauty and purity. I almost don't know who I am tonight.

"So don't make us wait. How did it go with Zane Blue?" Julius leans forward so he can see her, his elbows on his knees. Daisy smiles from ear to ear. I glance at Skylar, and she's staring at me, a quiet smile on her face. She caught me.

"It went great. We agreed to meet for lunch tomorrow. I'm so thrilled but nervous as hell."

"Congratulations," Lacey says. "Josh worked it for you."

I shake my head and lift my hands. "I hardly did anything. I introduced them, then walked around the gallery. She did it all on her own, and she was amazing." From the corner of my eye, I see her slip a mint in her mouth. Out of curiosity, I turn my head to observe Julius and Skylar. Do they know she does this? Maybe I have no right to focus on it at all.

"Wait, our train leaves at ten," Jocelyn says. "You'll miss it."

"Yeah. Can you take another one?" Sophia responds.

"I'm not going to miss this opportunity so, yes, I'll take a later train."

My turn. "I'm headed into the city too. Dais decided to take the train with me at four. I have a meeting on Monday, plus I'm getting my tuxedo fitted." I wink at Sophia. "I couldn't tell you how long it's been since I've worn a tuxedo." Everyone's eyes focus on us. I'm not going to bother saying anything else. I don't have the energy. They can think what they want.

"Good idea," Will slurs. "I already forgot that you were going tomorrow." I cock an eyebrow. We just discussed it this morning.

"Lace, did you guys drive here or did you get an Uber? I have my car—I can drive you home."

"We drove. Don't worry, I only had one glass of

wine at dinner." She pulls the beer out of Will's hand. "No more alcohol for you, buddy. We have to work in the morning."

"And we all have to get up early so we don't miss the train," Drew adds, standing up. "With that said, I'm going to bed." He reaches out his hand for Sophia to follow.

"Patti, do you mind if I leave my bags here until after my lunch meeting tomorrow?" Daisy asks. She's hiding her hands in her sleeves. I have this urge to take them between mine and warm them up. Better yet, pull her onto my lap and give her the hug she desperately needs.

"Sure. I don't have plans tomorrow. I'll be here."

We head into the house and everyone hovers by the front door to say goodbye. Once Lacey and Will leave, the others agree on when to meet for breakfast. Finally, Skylar and the rest wander upstairs, while Daisy and I wait for them to disappear. Patti walks in from the patio.

"Bye, Josh. Sleep well, Daisy."

"I guess that means I have to go," I mumble.

"It's probably for the best. I have a long day ahead of me. I need to sleep so I can win over Zane."

"Just call me when you're done, and we can figure out our plans for the train."

She opens the front door for me and leans her body against it. "Thanks for today. I had a lot of fun. I wish it didn't have to end."

"Anytime. Sleep well, butterfly." I want to hug her,

but I decide not to at the last minute. "See you tomorrow."

I find myself smiling as I head down the path. This was a most unusual day, but more fun than any day hanging out at the marina or with any of my friends lately. Daisy was afraid that I'd think differently of her because she's a recovering alcoholic. I do, but in a good way. She amazes me with her strength to change her life for the better. She's a genuine person and isn't looking to impress anyone. She just wants to be loved like everyone deserves.

I pat my pants pockets and realize I left my keys—and my sports bag—in Daisy's room. Shit. I turn around and walk back. All the lights are still on. Hopefully someone is still downstairs. I approach the door and look through the stained-glass windowpane. I can make out Patti walking around. I knock lightly and within seconds she cracks the door open.

"Oh, Josh, it's you. I got a little nervous. No one knocks at this hour."

"I'm sorry, Patti. I left my stuff in Daisy's room. Can I go up?"

"Sure."

I take the stairs two at a time and quietly walk to her room. With my ear to the door, I listen for movement, then my phone pings. I take it out and see a message from Daisy.

Daisy: You forgot your bag and the maple syrup.
Me: And my keys. I'm outside your bedroom door.

It creaks as it opens, and she laughs.

"I guess you need your keys to drive," she whispers. She opens the door wider so I can go in. It closes behind me. "I forgot you left your bag up here until I tripped over it while getting my pjs on." Because she said pajamas, I have to look at what she's wearing.

My heart hammers and my temperature spikes as my gaze traces the smooth lines of her body. She's wearing a blue cotton pajama set—short shorts and a spaghetti-strap top that reveals the natural curves and perfect size of her breasts. It teases me even more than the bikini. She looks softer, more petite, and alluring. My hands and lips ache to touch every twist of ivy on her body. *Will I ever have the chance?*

"Josh… you're making me blush again." I shake my head to snap out of it. "Do you enjoy doing that?"

I love it because, even though she's blushing, she's not trying to cover herself up either. Why is that?

"Actually, yes. But I can't help it right now. You look sexy as hell in that. So I need to leave now or I'll lose those five hundred bucks tomorrow. You're such a temptation, and you don't even know it."

She rolls her eyes and points to the door. "Okay, mister. You need a break. Turn off your flirt meter for the night and sleep it off."

"All right. I'm going." I pick up my bag and drag myself to the door.

She opens it, and we stand there staring at each other. We've done that a lot today. Every cell in my body wants to stay with her tonight. Not for sex. I just want to know what it'd be like to sleep next to her. To wake up with her. But I know I can't. I turn to leave, then turn back.

"Daisy, just so you know." I lean a little closer and whisper, "That wasn't me flirting just now. It was me being dead honest." She gasps, and I peck her on the cheek. "Sweet dreams."

She'll be the star in my dreams tonight. Maybe I'll be in hers.

15

DAISY

"Oh, come on," the passenger next to me complains loudly. "Why did we stop? It's hot as hell in here."

The conductor explains over the intercom that there's a train in front of ours with electrical problems. We can't move forward until that one is fixed or moved. Loud protesting erupts from the crowded train. Ours has issues too—there's no air conditioning. How long will we be stuck in this tunnel? At least everyone stays in their place. We don't want panic.

And of course, my stop is the next one. I remove my cardigan and drape it over my skirt. My Kindle will keep me company or I can just replay the fantastic last few days I've had.

Lunch with Zane went well yesterday, but it was cut short. We made plans to meet again today, then I traveled back to the city with Josh. When we got here, he took me to the Leonardo Grand where he's staying, to show me around. Sophia and Drew's wedding will be top-notch. We weren't allowed to go to the viewing deck because of the wind.

I didn't want the night to end, so I asked him if he wanted to see my place. While he was there, we ordered take-out. I got a little bit mellow when he talked about going to St. Thomas in January. The way he described the beauty of St. Thomas and the British Virgin Islands, why would he want to stay up here in the cold, dreary north during the winter?

He ended up staying until eleven. But after last night, I don't know when I'll see him again. It might not be until the wedding in two weeks. My heart aches, knowing it could be that long until I see his gorgeous face or hear the flirty tone in his voice.

This morning, I received a call from an artist that Skylar's gallery manager referred to me. When the call ended, I was stunned into silence. I've agreed to a video conference with her on Thursday, and if all goes well, we'll meet in Boston so I can see her paintings.

After that call, I had an appointment with my therapist to update her on my weekend. I thanked her because she encouraged me to let things go, and that's what I did. And I confirmed to her that I had the time of my life.

And then, just before I got on the subway, I finished an even more successful lunch meeting with Zane Blue, this time without interruption. He's agreed to take me on as his agent, and he's waiting for me to prepare the contract.

I am flying high right now.

The first person I wanted to call was Josh. Not even Julius or Skylar. Josh told me to call or leave a message with an update. I almost did, but reality took over and reminded me that the weekend is over. I had the best time, and I don't want anything to ruin it. He helped me come out of my shell, made me laugh, made me feel beautiful, and made me think I can do anything. But I'm back in New York, and he's going back to the Hamptons tomorrow. Back to real life.

Just call him. Fine. I'll send him a message when I get home. If I ever get out of this disgusting, sweltering train.

I turn on my Kindle and dive into my favorite author's latest book. The story is so engaging that I don't realize how much time is passing. When I look up next, we've been stuck in here for over thirty minutes. I glance up at the ceiling, then rotate my neck from side to side. Sweat trickles down my back, and the woman next to me seems to have forgotten to put on deodorant today. Or is it me? *Get me the hell off this train.* Good thing I'm not claustrophobic.

My eyes wander the train and inspect the different people around me. Most of them are on their phones. I catch an older man staring in my direction, but I'm not sure if he's looking at me. If he is, it's with complete disgust. It's a facial expression I'm all too familiar with but haven't seen since I was fourteen. I might lose my lunch.

I break eye contact, put my head down, and pretend to read. Movement at the corner of my eye alerts me, but I don't move. I mind my own business.

Suddenly, a pair of beat-up, dirty, old work boots stop next to me, and chills go up my spine. I smell his putrid breath, rancid from alcohol. The woman next to me nudges my side, but I keep my head down.

"Look at you," a voice hisses. "Covered in hideous tattoos. People like you are ugly and worthless. No one wants you. Not a man or a woman. Not even someone blind. You're a disgrace to society." Drops of spit land on the blank Kindle screen. He kicks my foot a couple of times. Not too hard but enough to scare me. There's some commotion and yelling.

I look up and my pulse explodes. My body begins to tremble. I embrace my handbag like it's the stuffed elephant I had when I was little. That same old man is standing in front of me, reeking of alcohol and cigarettes. The smell that takes me back to when my father was alive. *"You got nothin' to say, bitch? You're just like your fuckin' weak motha. Ain't no one's gonna want ya with your ugly pock-face and your fuckin' rotten buckteeth. My skin crawls looking at ya. The only man who'll ever want ya is the one who pays. But I don't know if they'd even want you. Guys I've offered ya to didn't want ya. You can't even earn me enough to buy a goddamn six-pack. You're an embarrassment to this family, just like your fuckin' freak brotha and lazy, miserable motha."*

I scream in my head to leave me alone as I crawl to the corner of the living room. Where's Julius? He usually saves me from him. From the devil. He always tells me to hide in the bathroom and lock the door. Where is he? Josh, help me!

"Miss, are you okay? He's gone, honey. The train is back up running, and we're arriving at the next stop." The woman next to me is tapping my shoulder gently.

I look up, and my nervous eyes scan the train. The asshole is gone. My award-winning smile disguises my imploding anxiety. The pounding of my heart in my ears won't quiet down. I'm overcome by an intense craving to drown my thoughts in something other than water. *Keep smiling*.

"I'm fine, yes. Thanks." I calmly place my Kindle back into my bag and slip my cardigan on, then drape my handbag across my shoulder so my arms are free. The air is so thick in here. *Breathe, Daisy*.

The train slows, and I jump from my seat, grabbing a handrail by the door. *Almost there*. It stops, and the doors slide open. I dart through, bumping into people. They yell at me, but I don't care. I find the stairs and run up as fast as I can. I'm through the turnstiles in seconds and run out of the station.

Cold, pouring rain douses my body. I welcome the relief, but it's not enough. As I gather my bearings, there's only one place I want to go. My body moves forward as if it's in control, not my mind. It knows what it wants, and it's taking me there. *Just one drink*. That's it. *Just one*.

I push through the door of the store and quickly find what I want. I throw money on the counter and don't even take the change. The bottle's in my bag, hidden from everyone. The cashier knew what I was doing. I could see it in her eyes.

I burst back through the door and dive into the crowds, forgetting that it's still pouring and I have no umbrella. The rain runs into my eyes and blurs my vision. I don't care, because I know what's waiting for me when I get to the penthouse… and it's not people. I can taste it on my tongue. It's what's in my bag. One more block. *Keep going*. Who cares how wet or cold I am.

Perfect timing. The entrance to my building opens, and my nosey neighbor, Candy, exits. I put my head down, hoping she'll leave me alone.

"Daisy, are you okay? You look frantic. Did something happen?"

I brush by her, mumbling, "I'm fine." She says something else but I ignore her. I pace back and forth in the elevator.

Don't do it, Daisy.

"But it's only one drink. It'll calm me down." The door slides open even slower than the train's did. I squeeze through it and rummage through my bag for the keys. I'm shaking like a leaf.

Don't do it.

"No one will know. It'll be my little secret."

I get the door open, drop the keys on the floor, and head straight to the kitchen. A few more seconds and the world will disappear for a little while. My father is still in my head. I remove the whiskey bottle from my bag with my shaking hands and stand it on the kitchen island. The bag drops from my fingers to the floor. I stare at the bottle and my mouth waters. I can already taste it on my tongue. *Just one drink*.

I strip off my soaked cardigan and toss it to the side. My body shivers profusely.

Don't do it.

I retrieve a glass from the cabinet and slam it hard on the counter, almost shattering it. I close my eyes and take a deep breath, gripping the bottle. I twist the cap open and rest it on the counter.

Don't do it.

Ignoring myself, I fill the glass, licking my lips in anticipation.

I twitch when my phone rings. "What the fuck?" My hand clenches the glass.

Just one drink.

The phone keeps ringing.

Answer it.

I shake my head.

Answer it!

Slowly, glass still in hand, I bend over to pick up my bag. The phone stops ringing. Relief takes over, and I look at the glass. The phone rings again. Startled, I grab it, turn it over, and see Josh's name. *Josh!*

I hit accept on the screen. "Josh!" I burst into tears. "Help me!"

Maybe he can't help me. Maybe it's too late.

16

JOSH

I couldn't help it. When I saw the store, I had to buy one. When Daisy and I said our goodbyes last night and promised we'd see each other at the wedding, I was gutted. And the strong urge to kiss her was there again, but we both kept our distance.

I don't want to wait until the wedding, and I don't think she wants to either. Why should we? I had more fun this weekend than I've had in a long while. Even going out with my friends hasn't been satisfying lately. Maybe I'm tired of going to bars and drinking all the time. After this weekend, I'd gladly hang out with Daisy over anyone else.

But the bet. *Fuck the bet*.

I pull out my phone. If she doesn't answer, I'll have time to wrap it. I tap on her name and listen to it ring in my ear. I shake my head. Voicemail picks up. I click call again by accident but who cares, maybe she didn't hear the phone.

"Josh!"

My stomach turns and I freeze, almost dropping my phone.

"Help me!"

"Daisy, what's the matter?" She's sobbing so hard, I can't understand her. But I know it's bad. I feel it in my bones. "Are you home?"

"Yes. Hurry."

"Call the front desk to let me up." I hear a soft *okay*. "I'll be there as fast as I can."

Keep her on the phone.

"You know what? Stay on the phone with me." A taxi pulls over as I lift my hand. I jump in and slam the door, then tell the driver to please hurry, it's an emergency. "Are you still there, Daisy?"

"Yes," she says with a quivering voice.

"Daisy, did you have a drink?"

"No, but the glass is in my hand," she admits.

Fuck! "Don't drink it. Don't do it. I'm on my way." I rub my thigh so hard there'll be a hole soon. "Wait for me. I'll help you. Did you call one of your friends? Julius?"

"No," she cries. "I saw your name on the phone, and I realized you're the only one I want to talk to. I'm sorry."

"Don't be. I'm glad I called." I look at the bag from the T-shirt store. Maybe what I bought will help her. "What triggered this?"

"My fucking father."

What? "Daisy, you told me your parents died years ago. I don't understand."

"He'll always be in my head," she whispers. My heart squeezes because I want to be holding her right now. Why can't Julius be home?

I tap the back of the driver's seat. "Hurry, please."

"I'm going as fast as I can. We're almost there," the driver responds.

"Tell me what happened, Dais. What triggered this?"

"Not till you get here."

"Where are you right now?"

"Sitting on the kitchen floor."

"Did you empty the glass and the bottle?" Silence.

The taxi comes to an abrupt stop. I throw cash at the driver and jump out.

"Daisy, I'm here. Buzz me up." She doesn't answer. I check my phone and the call was cut.

The door buzzes and I'm allowed through. I head for the elevator. Concern and confusion morphs the doorman's face. My body's tight, and my head is spinning. What will I see on the other side of the door? Once I'm out of the elevator, I run down the hall. The door is open.

"Daisy!" My eyes scan the open living room area and then the kitchen to the left. My throat closes when I find Daisy sitting on the floor with her back against the island. She's wet like she was caught in the storm that blew through. Her hair is matted down and her makeup has streaked down her face. She's shaking. A glass is in her hand, resting on the floor next to her. It's half empty. Did she drink it? She looks up and, when she sees me, she breaks into a million pieces.

My heart shatters. I run to her and kneel down. "Daisy, I'm here. You'll be okay."

"I'm sorry."

"Did you drink any of it?" She shakes her head. "Tell me the truth."

"I almost did. I was so close, but I won't let him fucking win."

"Who?"

"My asshole father."

I want to hold her but I have to get rid of the alcohol first. I touch her hands; they're freezing and wet. From alcohol or rain? I pry the glass free. She doesn't fight me.

"I'll be right back." I stand up, then I spot the large whiskey bottle. *Fuck!* I snatch it off the counter and want to throw it across the room. *Calm the fuck down.* I dump the contents from both and find a spot to put the bottle out of view. Throwing it out the window seems like a better bet.

I walk around the island and kneel down next to her with a wet towel. I wash her hands and wipe down the floor just in case something spilled out of the glass. She's staring ahead and looks depleted of energy. "Daisy, is this the only bottle you bought?"

She looks directly into my eyes and I know she's going to speak the truth.

"Mmhmm."

"Good." I kiss her forehead and touch her shoulder. Her clothes are soaked.

I rest one of her arms on my shoulder and scoop her up. She immediately wraps the other one around my neck, and I squeeze her tight. *Everyone needs human touch.* This feels right. I want to be here for her. I head down a hallway, looking for her bedroom. I find it and lay her on the bed. My knees crack as I kneel down, then I caress her face with the back of my hand.

"Daisy, you need to get into warm clothes... or do you want to take a warm bath? I can run it for you. Or a shower, maybe?"

She rolls onto her side, facing me. Her left hand disappears under the pillow. "Thank you for being here."

"I'm glad I called when I did. Call it fate." I tap her nose and a slight grin appears.

"Let me take a quick shower. I want to wash the last hours off my body. After that, I want to tell you everything." A small tear runs from the corner of her eye, over the bridge of her nose, then drips onto the blanket.

"There's no pressure, butterfly. You should sleep a little bit."

She embraces my hand and holds it against her chest. "It's sweet when you call me that. I trust you, and I want you to know all of me. Not little pieces of a puzzle."

"I want that too."

"I'm so tired of hiding." She sighs.

I rub her hip. "Take your shower, and we'll see how you feel after that."

She sits up slowly, then opens a drawer in the

nightstand next to her bed and pulls out a container of mints. Her hands are too shaky to open it, so I help her.

"How many do you want?"

"Three." I open her hand and drop them in her palm. She pops them in all at once.

"What can I do for you?"

"Please get rid of the whiskey bottle and rinse down the sink. I don't want to see or smell it."

"No problem." She tells me where the garbage goes in the building and where her keys are so I don't get locked out. Apparently, she tossed them on the floor somewhere near the door.

Once I hear the shower turn on, I rush to the kitchen. I get everything washed down and cleaned up in record time, then I perch on the couch in the living room, nervous as hell. Should I be in there with her? I check my phone and see some messages from Will asking about the meeting I had today. I'm not in the mood to respond.

"Hey," Daisy says softly from the hallway near her bedroom. She looks adorable in the tight black T-shirt and yoga pants she's wearing. Her blue eyes stand out even more against the dark clothing. Her damp blond hair is held back with a black headband. I stand up and meet her by the kitchen.

"Would you like something to eat? Or maybe some tea or water?" I offer, not knowing what else to do.

"You can relax in the kitchen with me for a

minute. I'll make myself some tea." She opens a cabinet and pulls out a wooden box full of different tea varieties. Once she finds the one she wants, she pulls it out. "Do you want some green tea too? I usually drink coffee, but I need something light for my stomach."

"Water's fine. I'll get it."

She opens a cabinet stuffed with several different types of glasses. "Take your pick."

I choose the first one I see and fill it from the faucet. For only two people living here, they have enough glasses for thirty.

She fills the electric kettle and turns it on, then takes a large teacup painted with red maple leaves and a matching saucer out of another cabinet. She exudes exhaustion, like her body weighs a ton. I observe her, staying out of her way as she moves quietly around the kitchen. A breeze of her fresh clean scent blows past me. I always like how she smells. It's never strong like perfume. Maybe a light body lotion or just her soap. Pure, like powder.

I wonder when she'll start talking. She places the cup in front of the kettle and hangs the tea bag over the edge.

"Thanks for cleaning the kitchen." I nod even though she's not looking at me. The water boils and the kettle turns off. She pours the water in and dips the bag several times. Finally, she turns toward and rests her lower back against the counter. Her face is sad, or maybe it's her eyes. The sparkle is gone.

"Did the shower help?"

"Yes. I don't feel like a zombie anymore. But you being here makes me feel a lot of different things." I eye her suspiciously.

"Only good things. You just saw me at my worst, and you're still here. And I'm not embarrassed. Well, maybe a little bit."

"Daisy, I'd never leave you. Anybody who would is a coward."

She rubs her lips together then picks up her cup with a shaky hand. She puts it back down on the saucer. "Let's go sit on the couch," she says.

She goes to lift her cup again but I stop her. "Let me take it for you." She nods, then I pick it up. "I don't want to see you burn yourself." I also grab the box of tissues on the counter and follow her into the living room.

I wait to see where she sits before I put the cup on the table. She gets comfortable at the far-left corner of the gray sectional. Her legs lie across the cushions. I put the cup down closest to her, then lift her legs and sit down, resting them over my lap. I want her as close to me as possible in case she falls apart again. I want to be the one who puts her back together. *Always*. I stuff the tissue box at her side for easy access and begin massaging her feet.

She takes a deep breath and exhales. "Mmm. That's nice." Her eyes close and her head falls back.

"Daisy, tell me what happened. Let it out. It'll help. You can tell me anything."

She raises her head and brushes her fingers along my upper arm. "I know, and you don't know how good that feels."

I rub her thigh to urge her to start talking.

"I had such a great weekend and today was awesome too... until I got on the subway to go home. I sat down with such a bright outlook. I'll tell you why later, if you still want to hear it."

"Stop it. Just talk."

"I found a seat in the crowded train and replayed all the good things that are happening in my life right now. Then we got stuck because there was another train ahead of us with electrical problems or something. There was no AC and people were bitching." She grabs a tissue from the box, and her hands start to shake again.

"Daisy, it's okay. I'm here. Nothing is going to happen to you."

"An—" Her voice cracks. "A crotchety old man came up to me, yelling about how disgusting my tattoos were and some other horrible things." She drops her head and sobs into her hands.

I can't take seeing her cry. I grab her waist, scaring her I think, and pull her over to sit on my lap. She's facing me, and her eyes are wide with surprise. A tear trails down her cheek. I wipe it away with my thumb.

"Sorry, I can't have you so far away from me when you're crying. This is better, right?" I slide a blanket off the back of the couch and wrap it around her shoulders. "Okay, keep going."

She pulls the blanket tight. "He was in my face, and suddenly it was like I was sucked back in time to my childhood. I was in our living room, listening to my drunk father shout about how hideous I was and how no man would ever want me. Telling me I was disgusting and no one would want to touch me because I had acne and bad teeth. That I couldn't even make enough money for him to buy him beer."

"What? Did he let people touch you?" My voice roars and my face burns.

She looks down and whispers, "Almost." Relief settles in but my anger is too potent to let it take over. "Men would show up at the house, and my father would bring me into the living room. As if showing them a prized possession. They circled me. It made my skin crawl." She shivers. "I want to throw up just thinking about it."

"How old were you?"

"Eleven or twelve. There was a lot of whispering between the guys and my dad. The two times that it happened, the men walked out. I didn't know why. I'm thankful he never found guys who were as evil as he was. But when they left, I just stood there shaking, because I knew what was coming next."

"Did he hurt you?"

Another tear falls. She gives a tiny nod. "But he was smart. He hit us where no one could see it. Never in the face. Most of the time, anyway. He also threatened that he'd hurt Mom or Julius if I told them about the men."

"Did you ever tell Julius later on?"

She shakes her head and looks down. "No. You're the only one. Not even my therapist knows. Please don't tell anyone."

I rub my hands through my hair and clench my jaw. A vision of my happy family flashes before me, and I can't for the life of me imagine any of this happening to me, Will, or Chloe. I've read stories about abusive families, but I've never met a person who's actually endured it.

I press her folded hands to my lips. "Your secret is safe with me. I promise."

"I know. Thank you." Her hands lower, but I don't let go of them.

"What else happened?" I say through gritted teeth.

"I don't remember a day of peace in the beat-up trailer we lived in. Constant fighting, yelling, and things breaking. Julius took the brunt of the beatings to protect me and Mom."

Now I understand why he's so protective of her. Not that I'm anything like their father.

"Julius was born with an eye disorder. It's color-blindness in its worst form. When he was diagnosed, he had to wear big sunglasses all the time due to severe light sensitivity. There's no cure, so he can only see black, white, and gray. So when my father"—her voice drips with acid on the name—"wasn't belittling me, it was Julius's turn. My father drilled it into all three of us that we were an embarrassment to him. He made me feel ugly in my own skin."

Her tattoos.

"We both ended up with insecurity issues and distanced ourselves from people."

"Where was your mom?"

"Working to pay the bills. When she was home and she knew he was drunk or that he was going to start, she'd send Julius and me outside to take pictures far away from the house. We knew that he beat her or took advantage of her against her will."

Fuck! If this is the only example of a husband and father she has, no wonder she hasn't dated much. She probably has no trust in men other than Julius.

"Daisy, how did your mom die?" I ask cautiously.

"She overdosed on antidepressants after a big fight with my father. He hit her hard in the face. I was fourteen, and Julius was sixteen. Julius got in the middle, then he yelled at me to go to the bathroom and lock the door. He told Mom to go to the bedroom and lock her door too. I should've gone with her into her room. Finally, I heard the front door slam, and things quieted down. Then Julius started screaming." Her voice cracks again, and she bursts into tears.

I wrap my arms around her because I know what's coming. She rests her wet cheek in the crook of my neck.

"I ran out of the bathroom and found Julius holding my mom, crying in the bedroom. He did everything he could, but by the time the ambulance came it was too late. Julius still feels guilty from that day."

I'm so fucking angry right now. If her father were still alive, I would go kill him with my own two hands.

And I'd gladly go to jail for it. I picture a young Daisy, powerless and fragile. I have a completely different view of Julius now.

"After that, it got even worse. Our father blamed us for Mom's death. You can imagine all the despicable things he said to us, and the beatings didn't stop. Well, not for Julius anyway. He protected me every chance he got. He slept in the same room with me and kept a bat next to the bed in case our father tried to come in, drunk and violent."

"When did your father die?"

She sits back up and wipes under her eyes, then blows her nose again. "A couple months later. He was drunk, riding a bicycle. He drove off the road and crashed into a ravine. It's sad and horrible to say, but that was the best thing that could've happened.

"Anyway, long story short, because I don't want to take up all your time…"

I take her chin in my hand. "Talk to me as long as you want. I'm not going anywhere."

"Social services wanted to split us up. Then, like an answer to our prayer, my father's sister came to our rescue. Thanks to my asshole father, we hadn't seen her since we were little. But Aunt Marie took us in to her house in Brooklyn as if we were her own children. Boy, was she a saint to take on two screwed-up kids. But she found a specialist that helped Julius with his eyes, and she gave us a warm, loving home to live in."

"Where is she now?"

"Sadly, she died too. She left us everything. That's how we could afford to buy this place. Well, Julius's success helped, but… When she died, Julius closed himself off again. Photography was his only outlet. Skylar broke the spell. It's a wonderful thing to see him so happy and in love. He's a good man and he deserves it."

"So you tattooed most of your body because of your father?"

"Yep. I couldn't look in the mirror anymore without hearing or seeing him belittling me. I hated my own skin, so I thought I could make it prettier and feel more confident."

"Do you feel that way?"

She bobs her head back and forth. "Yes and no. I can't change anything and get them removed. I don't know how my aged skin will look later. But I find them really pretty and purposely had the artist make them faint and delicate. I picked ivy because it's hardy and can live in the worst conditions."

Like her and Julius. I cup her face. "I think you're beautiful inside and out. And I'm not just saying that and this isn't me flirting. This is pure honesty."

She smiles. "That means a lot coming from you. I think you can see why dating is not a big thing for me. I never felt a connection with a man before, certainly not enough to give myself over to him. I've never slept with anyone.

"Just once, I'd like to be kissed and feel it through my entire body, like women talk about. I feel this strong connection to you. It's a feeling that lights me up when you're around. Ever since the barbecue, I've thought about you. After this weekend, I don't know if I'll ever be able to get you out of my head." Her face turns red, and she looks away. "I'm sorry. I shouldn't have told you that." She pulls away from me and tries to stand up, but I won't let her.

Maybe my future just became clearer.

"I'm sorry. I shouldn't have told you that." I push away from him and try to stand up, but he pulls me back down onto his lap.

"I'm not sorry, butterfly. I feel it too. At first, I thought it might be because you were off-limits because of the bet, but it's not. It's more. It's different. *You're* different. And it's not that I feel sorry for you. I care about you *a lot*, more than any woman I know. And after what you've told me and after what happened today, I have to admire how remarkably strong and courageous you are."

Hearing those beautiful words come out of his mouth makes my heart beat faster. *What if I fall in love with him?* No. I can't think about that now. *But what if I already am?*

"I know it's just been a short amount of time, really short—" He stops, and we both chuckle. Then he shakes his head. "But I've never enj—no, I've never connected emotionally with a woman like I do you. You've been on my mind a lot longer than this weekend. Ever since that day in August. But what can I offer you in a relationship? I'm only here until New Year's, and then I go back to St. Thomas. You deserve more than that."

I put my fingers to his soft, tempting lips. "Please don't talk about your leaving. I just want to enjoy this time with you, even if it's only for tonight or for a couple of days. You have no idea how beautiful and special you make me feel. I want to stay in this bubble right now. Just me and you."

He sits up straight and wraps his arms around me, pulling me against him. Our faces are so close that I can see a hint of fire in his eyes. Pulses of electricity pump through my veins, warming my entire body. "Is there anything else you want to tell me?"

"Nope."

His head angles to the side. "Are you sure?"

"Yes." For some reason that makes me smile.

"Good."

I wait patiently for his next words.

"Can I be the one who gives you that kiss?"

Every inch of me lights up like the Fourth of July. "Yes," I murmur.

His gaze traces my face like a soft feather, then he leans in and peppers sweet kisses along my jaw with his heavenly lips. I automatically arch my neck, holding back a moan. All the burning sensations I'm already feeling, and he hasn't even kissed me yet, are flowing straight to my core with such force. I can hardly breathe.

He kisses down my neck, teasing lightly with the tip of his tongue, then slowly kisses his way back up. "I love the way you smell and the taste of your soft skin." A lusty feeling of warmth embraces my heart.

Then his eyes capture mine intensely as if he's looking into my soul. The world as I knew it just minutes ago, disappears. This one kiss could change everything. I trail my fingers up his arms then place my hands on his chest, leaning into him, decreasing the space between us. I'm going to combust if his lips aren't on mine in a second. He gently wraps one of his large hands behind my neck, and I let my eyes flutter shut. The anticipation is killing me. His silky lips finally connect with mine, and I know I'm in heaven. All my fears and doubts melt away.

I part my lips and lick his, begging for more. He smiles against mine, then something clicks and his mouth is hungrily on mine as our tongues explore each other for the first time. He tastes sweeter than my favorite candy. There's no hesitation or awkwardness, just pure passion. He teases and nips on my lower lip, and that's when a moan does escape, and I don't care. My body wants to rub against his, but I refrain because this is supposed to be just a kiss. But I know in my heart and soul, it's so much more.

He pulls away and our eyes meet. I lean forward because I don't want it to end. His mouth takes mine again more possessively, and he combs his fingers through my hair. I wrap my arms around his neck. It's wild and heated, and I couldn't be any more surprised about how much better it is than I've imagined. I didn't think passion like this really existed until now.

I want us to go further. I want him to touch my bare skin. I want to feel his hard body against mine and in me, but I know it's not the right time. As if he feels what I'm thinking, we slow down and gradually part, sneaking in our last tiny kisses.

I lean my forehead against his, waiting to catch my breath. "All I can say to you is, *wow*. Now I know why the women lo—" He covers my mouth with his and sucks on my lower lip, then pulls away.

His hands caress my hips. "It's only you and me in this room. I'm not and don't want to think about other women. Understand? Being here with you is the only place I want to be. To tell you the truth, I think you've blinded me to all women."

"I know there's the bet, and you just lost."

"Daisy, this has nothing to do with the bet. I don't fucking care if I lost. I found you, and that's all that matters. *You* are the prize. But after what happened to you today, I think we should take it slow."

I curl up to him and lay my head on his chest. He wraps his arms around me. "You give good hugs too," I whisper. "It's going to be hard to let you go."

"You don't have to."

"Good."

We stay like this in silence, enjoying the warmth of our bodies together. He saved me today. Of all people, it was him. Telling him about my past makes me feel free. I was always hiding, and I don't feel like I have to anymore.

"I have an idea." I sit up.

"And what is that? Your face looks a bit sneaky."

"Don't tell Will and Lacey about this or us or whatever this is. It's something private between us. You or we can tell them at the wedding."

"Daisy, I would happily tell them about us. I told you, *I don't care about the bet or what anyone else says.*"

"Hear me out. I don't want to tell anyone because I don't have the energy to deal with people. I want to enjoy hugging you and maybe kiss you in between."

"I have to go back tomorrow. When will I see you again? I don't want to wait until the wedding." He rubs his strong hands up and down my legs. If we ever go beyond kissing, I'll go off in a snap. He would hardly have to touch me.

"How about Friday? Zane and I were talking about when we could review the contract I'm going to send him."

"Wait. He said yes? Congratulations." He kisses me, then hugs me tight. I want this to be a regular deal.

"Yes. I'm supposed to write up a contract this week. We had mentioned meeting to go over it on Friday. I can suggest that I go to him, and then I'll try to stay at the same place. I'd love to see Patti again."

"What are you going to tell Julius? He'll read right through it. Or even Sky."

I bite on my lower lip and take a deep breath. "I don't know. I'll tell him the truth. That I'm going to see Zane and maybe hang out with you. What would you say to Will and Lacey?"

"I have some friends that I hang out with on occasion. They can be my excuse. I don't want to lie, but I know where you're coming from." He pulls me flush against him. "It's kind of fun to be sneaky. I'm usually an open book."

My phone rings on the counter. "It's probably Julius. I'll text him in a little while."

"Are you going to tell him what happened today? I think you should. I understand why he is the way he is. I just wish he didn't think I was such an asshole."

"The only thing to worry about is what I think of you." I rub my lips against his, then pull away quickly. "Understand?"

"And you call me a tease. What the hell was that?"

"Want some more?" His eyes flash with desire.

"Fuck, yes."

Our lips claim each other, pouring all of our emotions out, setting our souls on fire.

Maybe I will get a happily ever after, after all.

18

JOSH

The bright morning sunlight shines through the windows, blinding me. I rub my dry eyes, trying to remember where I am. I turn to my left, and everything comes back in a sultry wave. Daisy lies next to me in her bed, sleeping peacefully. Last night, we talked, then ate dinner, then talked again. Kissing was involved, a lot, but we didn't go any further than that.

I lie on my side with my head propped up on my hand and observe her. It's impossible not to smile. Her rosy pink lips are parted slightly, and she has this unique little rumble or snoring thing going on. It's soft, so it's not annoying. It makes me believe she's in a deep sleep... maybe because I'm with her. Her long eyelashes rest perfectly on her flawless skin. As I breathe her in, I think about what it'd be like to wake up every morning with her in my bed. To hear her adorable giggle, to kiss her until she goes crazy, or to have her fall asleep in my arms at night. There's *never* been anyone in my life who I wanted to do these things with. Could I have a future like this with Daisy?

I flip onto my back and take a few breaths. Take it day by day. I don't want to fall in love with her—I'm leaving in a couple of months. She'd never do what Lacey has done. I wouldn't expect it. But why am I even thinking about falling in love with her? *Because you already are, idiot. No... Maybe... What?!*

I sit up carefully and look for a clock. My phone is in the living room. Her alarm clock says ten. My eyes widen. Thankfully, I have no meetings. I'm supposed to go to my dad's this afternoon. I need to pee, and I need a lot of coffee. I'll have to see if I can figure out her fancy coffee machine.

I tiptoe out of her room and close the door. I remember that I left the present for her in the living room too... or wherever my phone is. *Why didn't I give it to her last night?* Will is probably wondering where the hell I am since I never returned his messages. Daisy responded to one of Julius's.

I engage in a long battle with the coffee machine, but finally figure it out. Then I find my phone and text Will to say I'm fine and I'll call him later about the meeting I had yesterday. It was a good meeting, and I have something to pitch to Will and maybe even Lacey since they are a team. It could change everything.

In order for Daisy to see her present first, I put the bag on the island and place her phone on top. Then I text her to look in the bag.

Just as I'm pouring coffee into my cup, the front

door opens. In comes Julius. *Fuck!* Not good. My hackles go up, but why should they? We've done nothing wrong. I lean leisurely against the counter in the kitchen with my coffee cup in hand.

He places his luggage near the couch, still not noticing me in the kitchen. I put my cup down, then ease forward into the living room because I don't want him to wake Daisy by yelling or something.

"Hi, Julius." He jumps back.

"Josh?" His face turns red, and his fists ball at his sides.

What the fuck? Am I that terrible?

"What the hell are you doing here? Where's my sister?" He glances over my shoulder, then down the hall toward the bedrooms.

"She's sleeping, so keep your voice down," I demand under my breath.

"Why are you—?" He stomps toward me and gets in my face. I don't flinch. "Did you sleep with my sister?"

"Her name is Daisy. And technically, I did sleep with her, but I was wearing this outfit the entire time. You can see by the wrinkles on my trousers." I look down at them. He's going to punch me.

"Again, why the fuck are you here?"

"She almost had a relapse yesterday."

"What?" he yells. "What happened? Did you do something to her?"

I could slug him right now.

"Keep your fucking voice down and get out of my face. Can you for once stop pointing the finger at me or thinking that I'm the worst person your sister could interact with?"

He backs off and crosses his arms. "Then change my view of you."

We stay in this face-off position in the living room while I tell him in short detail what happened on the train and how she answered the phone when I called.

"She didn't drink anything?"

"No. She said she didn't and I believe her. I got rid of the bottle and cleaned up the kitchen so she wouldn't smell anything." I pause and take a breath. "Julius, she told me everything. About your father and mother."

His clenched jaw ticks to the point I think his teeth are going to crumble into little pieces.

"That's none of your fucking business," he growls. I laugh in his face.

"That's where you're wrong." I point at him. "It is my fucking business when I see Daisy falling apart in front of me, almost letting two years of being dry shot to hell because of your asshole father. I called just in time. If I hadn't, I don't know if she would've drunk that stuff or not. By the end of the night, she was smiling. Can you give me some fucking credit? I care for Daisy a lot, and I don't give a shit whether you like me or not. But I'd think you'd consider thanking me because I was here for her when no one else was. Or let me repeat what she said—I was the *only one she wanted* to help her."

"She has her friends or me to call when something like this happens. Not someone like you, that she's only known for a few days," he spits, puffing his chest out.

I shake my head. "You're unbelievable. Make excuses all you want. You want to hate me for no apparent reason, do it. But I understand why you're so protective of her and I can't thank you enough for that. I can't fucking imagine what you two have been through. Daisy needs you on her side. Now I understand why Sky loves you so much. But don't you dare look at me like I'm the bad guy or… like your damn father. Hell, I'm no saint, but I'm not looking to screw Daisy and walk away a second later, nor do I want to ruin all that she's achieved."

Julius's flinty stare bores into me, but it doesn't intimidate me. He begins to roll up one of his sleeves, his face remaining cold as ice without a flicker of resignation.

"Daisy and I had fun this weekend, and she impressed the hell out of me with Zane. Then with her confiding in me with her drinking and the horrific past you share, and how much she's overcome—she's the strongest and most beautiful woman I know. So pardon fucking me if I want to be a part of Daisy's life. And it's *her* choice who she wants to be with. Not yours and not mine."

"What the hell is going on here?" Daisy yells. Julius and I turn swiftly in her direction. The way she's standing, stone-faced and arms crossed, she's pissed.

Maybe with me or Julius or both of us, I don't know.

19

DAISY

*S*omeone like you, that she's only known for a few days... I lift my head off my pillow. Was that Julius? *Make excuses all you want. You want to hate me for no apparent reason, do it.* Yep. And that was Josh.

Shit! Julius is home. I forgot he was coming back early this morning. I hop out of bed and push my hair back.

But don't look at me like I'm the bad guy or... like your damn father. Oh, shit.

I run out of my room and stop short. They are like two bulls going head-to-head. I cross my arms and stand firm on the ground. "What the hell's going on here?" I say loudly. Both of their heads turn swiftly in my direction.

Julius approaches me, his heated anger melting to concern. He puts his hands on my arms. "Daisy, I'm sorry I wasn't here to help you. Are you okay?" I loosen his light grip on my arms and walk around him to the living room. I crack a smile at Josh and stand next to him.

"I'm much better. Josh helped me, and I would appreciate that to be your focus, Jules. It was fucking horrible, and he helped me get through it. I will never be able to repay him for that." I wrap my arms around my waist to keep myself from touching Josh.

"Daisy, I think it'd be best if I go so you two can talk alone," Josh offers.

"I do too," Julius adds snidely.

"Julius!" I bark, anger brewing in my chest. "Back off, or I'll walk out with him." His eyes flash but he remains firm in his stance. He's so damn stubborn.

"Josh, you don't have to leave. I don't want you to go," I say, pleading with my eyes.

His arm rises but then he quickly lowers it. After last night, it's hard for us not to touch each other. At least for me anyway.

"I should, though. I need to go to the hotel to check out and get my things." He wanders over to the kitchen and grabs his phone and wallet off the counter, then heads for the door.

"Josh, wait!" I run over and jump into his arms. He doesn't protest and wraps his arms around me, burying his face in my hair. "Thank you so much for last night. You know how much it meant to me." We pull away from each other.

He skims my cheek with his finger. "I know, butterfly. I'll always be here for you, no matter what. Good luck with Julius." He leans close to my ear. "Call me."

I open the door and let him out. I watch him walk to the elevator and get in. He waves as the door closes in front of him. Warmth fills my heart, remembering last night.

"Daisy," Julius calls behind me.

The warmth dissipates, and anger replaces it. *Keep your cool.*

I turn around slowly and walk back into the living room, stopping at the end of the sectional. "What?" My voice reflects no love.

He drops his chin to his chest, then a few seconds later he looks up. "I don't want to fight with you. I just want to know you're okay. Can I do something for you?"

I cackle. "Yes, you can. Back off when it comes to Josh. He's a good man, and he proved that last night."

His lips purse, and he rakes his hands through his hair. Typical reaction when he's irritated. "It freaks me out that I wasn't here for you. That you had to deal with it by yourself."

I throw my hands in the air. "Do you hear yourself? I wasn't alone! Just because you weren't here, doesn't mean I was by myself."

"I'm sorry. It's always been you and me. I'll always be protective of you. Always."

"Not that Josh is my boyfriend, but how would you like it if I treated Sky like you do Josh? There's no reason for you to treat him like shit."

"He's no good for you. He's always with different women… He likes to party and it doesn't look like he has any intention of settling down. How can a man like that fit into your life?"

Deny your feelings for him, Daisy, but you know he has a point.

"All I'm going to say is you don't see the side of him I saw this weekend and last night. If he were just out to get me in bed, he would've done it and walked away… bet or no bet. We forgot about our day-to-day lives and had pure innocent fun. Something I'm not used to having."

"Can you trust him to be quiet with the stuff you told him about our parents? Are you going to tell the others about your drinking problems?"

"You know what's funny? Telling him everything might have been the best thing I've ever done. I don't have to hide anymore. I woke up this morning with such a sense of relief. Telling someone other than my therapist was life changing for me. I shouldn't have to hide. *We* shouldn't have to, Jules."

"Do you think being around alcohol this weekend triggered something too?"

I shrug. "I don't know. It wasn't easy. I think I ate two packets of mints. That's not the environment I'm used to. Why do you think I sat at the front of the boat with Josh? You're worried about me being around him if he's drinking, but you and Sky were doing it all weekend. What's the difference?"

He drops onto the couch, then scratches his jaw. "I'm sorry, sis. There's no excuse."

"I'm not sorry, Jules. Now that we have friends outside our little circle—new friends that I love and who are like family—I have to get used to being around alcohol of some kind. And I can't expect people to change their habits just because of my issues. It'll be a challenge for me for the rest of my life. But I'd rather be around the people I love than live like I've been living.

"Yesterday was a huge wake-up call. Our father almost won again. Before Josh got here, I almost gave in. It took everything out of me not to chug that glass or the bottle. I was at breaking point. *It was in my hand.* Josh called just at the right time, and that woke me up. I refuse to let others or a substance control my life ever again."

I take a seat on the couch, twist toward him, and pat his leg. "Thank you for caring, but you need to adjust your attitude. Whether it's Josh or another man I bring home, could you please give me the benefit of the doubt? It's my choice who I want to be with."

"It'll be hard. You'll always be my priority."

"And you're used to me relying on you—it's what I've done my entire life. And I'm talking about my job too. This is where things need to change. Our lives are going in two different directions now. Even our living arrangements aren't ideal anymore. I'm thirty-one and still living with my brother. And his girlfriend is practically living with us."

He sighs heavily. "I know. I've been trying to avoid it. A lot of change in a short amount of time makes me twitch... you know that."

I chuckle and wrap my arms around him. "I love you, Jules. When the time comes, we'll figure it out."

Julius's phone starts ringing, and this conversation is over. He looks at the screen, then stands up. "I have to take this. It's probably about the shoot tomorrow. Can you still help out today and tomorrow or do you need some time to yourself?"

"Sometimes being alone makes me think too much. I need the distraction, and it's part of my job to help you. Let me shower, and I'll meet you in the studio."

He nods, then swipes his phone. "Hi, Cameron…" He disappears into the studio.

Well, that was one way to wake up. Not the way I wanted to. It would've been nice to wake up with Josh still in my bed. My phone pings over in the kitchen. I drag my feet over and yawn into my hand.

My phone is lying on a plastic navy-blue bag. Strange. Instead of looking at my messages, I put the phone aside and open the bag. What the hell? I stick my hand in and pull out the material. A plain white T-shirt? I turn it around, and tears threaten to form. Josh had a T-shirt made for me! The black lettering across the front announces: *My proudest moment was when I stopped.* How or when did he do this? And so fast.

I plant my ass on a kitchen stool and read it over and over again, tracing the words with my fingers. This phrase means even more today than it did on Saturday. He's the most thoughtful person. How did I get so lucky? An idea pops into my head.

I hurry to my room and put the shirt on, then stand in front of my floor-length mirror. Perfect fit, and it makes my boobs look good. I don't have a bra on but the letters cover my nips. Hopefully it's not too noticeable. I don't care. He saw me yesterday and this weekend without one.

I take a selfie of me wearing it with a big smile on my face. Just before I hit send, I add a red heart to the image.

My life starts fresh right now.

Maybe Josh came into my life for this one moment, or maybe more.

20

JOSH

I've spent the last hour sitting in the Leonardo Grand café, people watching and drinking coffee like water. My phone was ringing nonstop, and messages were pinging or binging... whatever the word is for that damn sound. I keep going over in my head everything that has happened since Friday.

I'm not an emotional guy. I don't cry often. The most I've ever cried is when Mom died and when my friend Sawyer's wife died. But last night when I saw Daisy at her worst? Yeah, I almost cried. I've never been so scared in my life. What if I couldn't have stopped her, what if I was too late? What would a relapse mean for her? I know it's something she'll battle with the rest of her life. With the feelings I have growing for her, I have to ask myself, could I handle it?

My lifestyle is different than hers. I drink alcohol and I'm surrounded by people who do too. Could it work between us? Can she live with the way I live my life? Could I live with *her* lifestyle?

But I'm leaving in a couple of months—why am I even thinking about long term? *Because my heart is involved.* It's already connected to Daisy's.

My phone dings again, and I'm ready to throw it at the first waiter who walks by. I push my now cold coffee to the edge of the table. The guests sitting around me are all on their phones or computers, making me feel guilty. Fine… I'll check my messages.

The smile that stretches the skin on my face is the best feeling. And this is just from seeing Daisy's name. But what if it's a bad message? When I left her place, the tension was sky high. I don't want to be the cause of her fighting with Julius.

I close my eyes and click on the message. It opens, and I take a peek. Relief takes over any questions or doubts I have. The picture of her wearing that T-shirt beats the one by the pool. My body instantly reacts. *Down, boy.* She didn't write anything, but the heart says it all. Even if nothing else happens between us, this weekend was worth it. I save the picture to the Daisy file I've created.

"Josh, what a surprise! What are you doing here? No work today?" My sister Chloe walks around the front counter and pulls me in for a hug. "How was the weekend? Crazy with the gang there?" She waves for me to follow her into the workroom at the back of the store.

The room is filled with every kind of flower you can imagine. There's hardly any open space to stand. A massive worktable in the middle of the room is covered with flowers and greenery, clippers, ribbons, vases, and glue sticks. It reminds me of the day Will surprised Lacey with a shitload of peonies. The things that love makes you do. *I know that firsthand. Wait. What?*

"Earth to Josh?"

I shake my head. "Oh! It was a lot of fun. Everyone missed you. I wish you could've been there."

She opens the refrigerator full of different varieties and colors of flowers, then pulls out several long-stemmed bright pink roses, shaking the water off the edges. "You and me both. All work and no play. But I guess it means my floral business is going well. Not sure how I'll keep up. I might need to hire another person."

"Well, you are one of the most sought-after florists in New York. Don't overdo it, though."

She laughs. Pieces of the stems drop to the ground as she clips the bottoms. "I'm looking forward to Drew and Sophia's wedding because I get to attend it. Yes, I'm doing the flowers, but once they're delivered and set up, it's party time. I'm closing the shop on Sunday to take a breather."

"Good for you. It should be a blast with Sophia's family coming over from Germany. She tells us they are quite the partiers."

"So who's your plus-one? I'm going alone. I went on a date the other night, and it was a waste of time. I left before dessert was served. Sometimes, you're just better off alone."

Not when you have someone like Daisy.

"No date for me either." *Liar.* "You never know who'll be there." I wiggle my eyebrows, and she snorts.

"Of course, Mr. Bachelor. New woman every other day."

She obviously doesn't know about the bet. I've kind of forgotten about it and, again, I don't care if I win or lose. Daisy isn't someone to fuck with.

"Anyway, what's the real reason you came here? You seem kind of down."

"Come over here for a second." She squints, unsure of what I'm going to do. I roll my eyes. "Just come here." I point to the spot next to me.

"Fine." She stands in front of me. I embrace her and squeeze her tight. She squeaks and stands still, then relaxes, hugging me back.

"What is this for?"

"I've experienced some crazy stuff recently... it really made me appreciate our family. I realized I don't tell you enough how much I love you. I'm always here for you if you need anything."

She pulls away a little bit. "This is quite the surprise. I love you too, big brother. I don't know what happened, but I hope you're okay."

"It didn't happen to me. The person is fine now, but it really shook me up and made me realize how lucky we are as a family and to have the parents that we do… or did."

She lets go of me and steps behind the worktable again. "It must have been pretty bad for you to do this. But I love that you're here. I miss seeing you guys. I dread that you're leaving again in a couple of months. Six months goes way too fast. Will you ever think to stay up here for good?"

"You never know what the future holds."

"Amen to that."

"Anyway, I have to go. I'm off to Dad's. But can you do me a favor? Can you wrap up some flowers for me? I want to visit Mom's grave."

Once I'm out of the shop, I take a selfie of me with the flowers and send it to Daisy.

> **Me**: Love the T-shirt on you. It fits perfectly in all the right places. I'm on my way to my dad's. The flowers are for my mom. I'm going to visit her grave today.

I hit send and wonder why I'm even telling her that. I'm surprised when she answers right away.

> **Daisy**: This shirt is so special to me. I will wear it until it literally falls off from being worn too much. Thank you. As for going to your mom's grave, I wish I could go with you.

Me: I wish you could too. It feels so natural to say that to you.

Daisy: Let's not question it. I love that you feel that way, and I'll take what I can get. I have to go. Julius is working my ass off today. He has a big shoot tomorrow. I need to keep busy so I don't think about you too much.

Daisy: Or your delicious kisses.

Daisy: Sorry, I had to throw that one in there. I'm on fire just thinking about them.

I am too.

Me: Get back to work before your brother has another reason to hate me. Talk to you soon.

I take a bus to Dad's, and by the time I finally make it there, I'm physically and mentally exhausted. I spent the time texting back and forth with Will and some of our employees. The flowers are probably crushed by now. I knock on the front door and walk in.

"Dad?" No response. I set my bag by the sofa, then walk through the house calling his name. I walk out of the house and notice how red Mom's favorite Japanese maple tree is. Daisy said maple trees are her favorite, so she'd love it. I take a picture for her. Boy, am I turning into a sap. A high-pitched whine from the electric saw running in the detached garage hints at where he is. Of course, it's his favorite place. Dad loves to fiddle with wood and build things like tables, benches, or even rocking chairs.

I push open the side door and cover my ears against the noise. Sawdust is shooting everywhere. My dad looks up and stops the saw, then takes off his safety gear.

"Josh! I lost track of time. It's three already?" He wipes the dust off his clothes. "Ah shucks, are those flowers for me?" he jokes. "You didn't have to." I forgot I still had them in my hand.

"Haha." We hug and pat each other on the back. "I know you're busy, but d'you want to go somewhere with me? I need you to drive, though."

"Sure. Let me clean up a bit."

Before too long, he's stopping the car near Mom's grave. "I'll tell you, son, this is not what I expected."

We get out of the car, and I'm thankful I have a jacket on. It's amazing the difference in temperature from this weekend. I don't say much as we walk to the grave. When we get to her plot, I unwrap the red roses and place them in front of the gravestone. Then I shove my hands in my pockets.

"Want to tell me why we're here? Something wrong?"

I shrug my shoulders. "Believe it or not, I come here almost every time I visit you. I've just never told anyone."

"Hmm," is all he says.

"I miss Mom a lot. I know I don't talk about her often. It hurts too much."

Dad places his hand on my shoulder. "Everyone

grieves differently, Josh. I never questioned whether you missed her or not. We all miss her—she's irreplaceable. I hope you and Chloe find the kind of love that your Mom and I had. Will's lucky to have found Lacey."

I look sideways at him and take a big breath. "What if I have found her, but I won't let my heart admit it? Our lives are complicated, and I don't know if they could match. Moving back to St. Thomas won't help. I haven't known her for too long, but during the short amount of time I've spent with her, my life has changed. I see everything differently. She's reminded me how important having a good family is. Her mom passed away too.

"I don't tell you enough how much I love you, Dad. You and Mom were the best parents. You gave us a warm, loving home. You adopted Chloe and gave her a life full of love after her mom gave her up in Africa. I'm so thankful for our family."

Dad puts his arm around my shoulder and pulls me to his side. "Wow, this woman must be really special for you to talk openly like this. It's unlike you. I always wondered if I'd ever see you like this, but it's okay. More than okay. You know, when I met your mom, I was a mental mess. But I knew immediately that she was the one for me."

I cock my head. "How?"

"It's hard to explain. You just know in your heart. It's as if it's whispering to you. I know it sounds corny, but we connected instantly and I could've spent every waking hour with her. I tried to hide it because I didn't want to scare her away." We chuckle. "But everything felt different. It scared the shit out of me because I was a player like you. But I never looked at another woman like I did your mom from the moment I met her. I haven't since she died either. Oh, and she didn't put up with my shit. I loved that about her. And we laughed all the time. It's so important. Does this woman make you laugh?"

"More than anyone."

"If she's making you feel like your head is in the clouds and you laugh a lot…" He gives me a sideways man-hug. "I'd say she's a keeper. But you're the only one who can tell. Just follow your heart and don't listen to anybody else. It's your choice. Remember that. This world's difficult enough. Finding the love of your life makes it bearable."

"Thanks, Dad. You always know what to say. Don't tell anyone about this. I have to work it out myself. Not Will or Chloe. It's between you and me."

"You got it, son. Why don't we go out for a big steak dinner tonight?"

"Sounds good to me. Remind me to tell you about a bed and breakfast the gang stayed in last weekend. You should stay there once. I think you'd love it."

I chuckle to myself. Since when am I a match-maker, with my dad no less? This love stuff really screws with you. We'll see if he'll take the bait. Stranger things have happened. Look at me and Daisy. After a couple of days of being with her, I'm already looking into the future, and it feels damn good.

As we walk to the car, I open my phone and send the maple tree picture to Daisy.

Me: Thinking of you. Thought you would like this.
This was Mom's favorite tree in our yard.

I don't expect a response. It's just to make her smile and know she's on my mind. But when we get back in the car, I say to Dad, "Want to see a picture of her?"

My heart isn't whispering, it's shouting. Maybe I should listen.

21

DAISY

"**K**nock, knock," Skylar says as she opens the front door to the penthouse. "Anybody home?"

"I'm in the kitchen making a smoothie," I call out to her. "Want some? You can be my guinea pig."

I scan the list of ingredients I need for a new veggie smoothie recipe I have. Spinach, cucumber, avocado, banana, flax seed, and almond milk. Check, check, check… I drink the last sip of my coffee and put the cup in the sink.

Skylar tosses her bag onto the couch and joins me in the kitchen. "Veggie smoothie, huh? You're such a health nut. I'll give it a try." She pulls out a stool and sits at the island.

I put a cutting board and the blender on the counter. My phone pings. I glance behind me to where it is. Josh's name flashes and warm tingling sensations form in my chest. He sent me a picture with something red. I open the message and I couldn't hide my smile if I tried. A red maple tree. I'll say it again... adorable. Thankfully, I've got my back to Skylar. He's so sweet for thinking of me. I'll respond later. I turn back around.

"You're here earlier than usual. Slow at the gallery today?"

"Yes. My assistant, Tori, offered to run the show for the rest of the day. I'm tired." She reaches over and steals a banana slice. I slap her hand away. She crosses her eyes at me, then looks closer at my chest. "What's your shirt say?" I stretch it out so she can read it.

"'My proudest moment was when I stopped'?" She looks puzzled.

"Josh bought it for me." My cheeks start to sizzle. "After I told him about my alcohol problem, he said this to me, and I mentioned it would make a great T-shirt. So here it is. When I have a hard time, I can look at this or wear it to help me get through it."

I'm just waiting for her to bring up last night. There's no way Julius didn't tell her. Hell, I'll just bring it up myself.

"He saved me yesterday, Sky. After he left this morning, I found this T-shirt in a bag waiting for me to open it. He had that made before he even knew I was in trouble. Just when I needed someone the most, he called at that very moment to see if he could bring it to me. He's a blessing in disguise," I babble, avoiding her gaze.

"Daisy, Julius told me everything. It must have

been horrible. I'm so sorry. But when it comes down to it, I'm glad you got through it… with Josh's help."

"He's a good guy. Better than most. Of course, Julius wasn't happy about him being here all night. But what happened yesterday was about me, not Josh. Julius only focuses on him, and that pisses me off like no one's business. I was at my worst in two years, and I still didn't have that drink. Would I have if Josh hadn't shown up when he did? I'd like to think not, but I don't know."

"Well, you didn't… and you should be proud. You really look and sound amazing, considering what happened."

"I am." I confirm it with a smile as I pour the almond milk into the blender. I add a bunch of spinach and then the banana slices. Now the avocado. I hate cutting them, but it keeps me busy so I don't have to look at her. "In a way, last night was the best thing that has ever happened to me. Telling Josh about my past was pivotal. I've let it control me for too long, but I'm not going to hide anymore. And I shouldn't have to—not my past or my alcohol problems." I toss the avocado pit in the trash. "What's crazy is that I think this helped me more than years of therapy."

"I'm happy for you that something positive came out of the situation. How did Josh react?"

"As caring as could be. He held me the entire time and let me cry as much as I wanted. He probably has boogers all over his shirt." I giggle. "I saw a side of him I don't think any of you have ever seen before or ever bothered to see. He makes me feel safe. We fell asleep in my bed after talking all night. He's probably exhausted like I am."

"Only talking?" She cocks an eyebrow.

"Even if there were more, it's nobody's business."

She presses her lips together, and I huff.

"He slept above the covers with the clothes he had on his back when he arrived." But my body tingles and butterflies swirl in my belly, remembering his soft lips on mine.

She looks at me for another minute, then nods with a hint of a smile. "Julius has the best intentions. I have a feeling it's hard for him to see you looking to someone else instead of him. You're both becoming more independent, and it's going to take time to get used to. I'll talk to him, see if I can reason with him. He's being a bit of a hardhead. You guys have gone through a lot of change, just in the time I've known you. He found me, and you've both gained a new family and friends. Going from being on your own to having all these new people around you is hard to get used to... I know it's not easy. This situation with Josh; it's another change."

I drop the avocado and flax seeds into the blender, cover it, and turn it on. It's a good break because I don't want to talk about this anymore.

I turn off the machine. We both look at the smoothie. "It doesn't look so bad. The light green color makes it look refreshing." I take two small glasses from the cabinet and pour a sample into each one. "Let's try it at the same time."

We each choose one, then we take a sip. We smack our lips together, tasting it on our tongues, trying to decide if we like it or not.

"Hmm," she says thoughtfully. "It's okay, but wasn't the cucumber supposed to be in there too?"

"Oh, shit, yes. Let me add it. It'll probably taste so much better." I grab the cucumber and start peeling. "So Zane Blue wants me to be his agent. I have to write up the contract tonight."

"Oh my gosh, Daisy. That's fabulous. Does Julius know? If he does, he didn't tell me."

I tell her about the first part of the day yesterday, before the shit went down. She's grinning like a Cheshire cat.

"I'm so thrilled for you. I wish we could show his paintings at my gallery, but we only deal in photography."

"Let's not get ahead of ourselves," I warn. "He hasn't signed the contract yet. I'm going to see him on Friday to discuss it in detail. Maybe he'll sign it right then. I'm really excited about working with art other than photography. I want to use my other skills and knowledge."

"Awesome, awesome."

"And I can't believe that other artist called, the one your boss knows. We have a video conference call set up for Thursday. Wouldn't it be a miracle if I got two new clients, one after the other?"

"We visited with Monica yesterday morning, and Julius mentioned you were looking for new clients. One thing led to another, and here we are."

"I need to call her and say thank you."

Just as I say this, Julius walks through the door from the studio.

"Hey, handsome." Skylar walks over to meet him. He kisses her softly on the lips like they haven't seen each other in days, and it hasn't been more than eight hours. My thoughts drift to Josh because I wish I could see him again today. I still need to confirm that meeting with Zane for the Hamptons on Friday, but I'll work something out.

"Daisy, I wanted to ask you something," Skylar says. I push the button on the blender and smirk. I turn it off.

"Sorry, what did you want to say?" She opens her mouth and I do it again, then turn it off. "Just playing with you. What did you want to ask me?"

"Jocelyn, Lacey, and I want to buy a special gift for Sophia for the wedding. We're going shopping on Monday since the gallery is closed. Lacey's coming Sunday night to spend Monday with us. Then maybe go to lunch. Oh, and then stop at Jocelyn's work so we can try on our bridesmaids' dresses one more time before the big day. Want to go with us? It should be fun."

"Let me look at my calendar and I'll let you know."

"Sure. Maybe you can help us think of what to get her. Jewelry is out of the question for obvious reasons. Drew would kick our asses if we bought something at a jewelry store other than his. She has enough already anyway. You should see the wedding bands he designed for them. Usually Jocelyn is good at gift ideas, but even she's stumped."

I bite the inside of my mouth. "If I go with you on Monday maybe I'll tell the girls about my drinking. I need to get it out there."

Surprisingly, Julius speaks first. "I think it's a good idea."

"I think so too," Skylar agrees.

My phone goes off. It's been nonstop today. Mostly because of Julius's shoot tomorrow.

Maybe it's Josh.

22

JOSH

"Butterfly, we should do video calls more often. It's good to see your happy face. I wish I could see it in person, though." Being alone in the office makes it easier for us to video call. I prop my phone up against my laptop screen so I'm hands-free. "Where are you? The bathroom?"

"I'm running a bath." She twists her phone quickly to show me the bubbles in the water. My heart skips a beat just thinking of her naked body beneath them.

"You called me right now to torture me, didn't you?" I growl.

"Maybe, maybe not. I'll never tell." She flashes me a sparkly grin. "I don't want Julius or Sky to overhear me. Not that I think their ears are stuck to my bedroom door, but I kind of like being secretive." She lowers her phone. "See, I still have your T-shirt on. It's a little snug in the chest. I have to wonder if you did that on purpose." Her face appears on the screen again.

"I had to guess your size. Do I get to see you in it this weekend? Did you confirm your meeting with Zane?"

"Aw. Do you miss me already?" She flutters her eyelashes. "Even after I was a crying mess last night." I want to jump through the phone and kiss her beautiful pink lips to show her how much I miss her.

"You tasted nice and salty from your tears. Did I ever tell you I prefer salty over sweet?"

"I'll have to remember to bring a bag of chips with me on Friday."

"I'd prefer you over anything else." She shakes her head and the giggles come out to play. "Why are you so red?" I ask playfully.

"Maybe I'm blushing or maybe it's from the steam building up in here. You'll never know." She winks at me. "But to answer your other question, yes, I've confirmed a meeting. I've already booked a room at Patti's for one night. Listen to me, I act like I know her personally. But that's her personality. She treated us like family."

"Can you stay the weekend? I don't think one night will be enough for me." I'm hesitant to ask her this, but I need to tell her something that's on my mind.

"Sure, but how are you going to get out of work? I don't want you to lie to Lacey and Will. Or Julius. Wait, don't answer that. Give me a second."

She places her phone down and the ceiling of the

bathroom comes into view. Shuffling comes through the phone. What the hell is she doing? Suddenly I hear the swish of water. I close my eyes. Do not tell me she's now in the bathtub.

The phone moves again and her heart-shaped face appears. "Okay. I'm ready. Sorry about that."

"Are you in the bath now?"

"Why?" she says coyly.

"You can't be doing that to me." The phone moves again, making me dizzy. She provides a view showing the mile-high bubbles and her little toes wiggling above the surface at the end. "That's not fair. And you say I'm a tease," I yell into the phone, adjusting my jeans. It's getting a little too painful in there.

Her face appears again. "I have a good teacher." An amused smile appears.

I need to get serious. "I want to tell Will and Lacey about us." Her eyebrows shoot up to her hairline. "Is that so bad?"

"No, no. I'm just thinking about the bet."

I sit up in the office chair. "Daisy, forget about the bet. I want to tell them because I don't want to hide it. We aren't in high school. They can have their five hundred dollars. I want to see you."

"What should I tell Julius?" With a wet hand, she pushes her hair away from her face.

"Tell him on Sunday when you get back. I don't care who knows. Not that I know what's happening between us."

"Whatever it is, I hope there'll be a lot of kissing

involved. And maybe other things…" As her voice trails off, she rests her head back on the tub, revealing the skin I tasted just last night. A flame of desire swirls through my veins.

"I can arrange that. Anyway, what do you say? I'd invite you to stay at my place instead of the B&B, but no way in hell with Will and Lacey being there. I'd rather be alone with you."

"Oh, so now you think you can sleep in my room? That's awfully presumptuous of you." She taps her cheek with her finger.

"What can I say, I go after what I want. And that is you."

"Until January," she mumbles in a tone I don't like.

No. Forever.

I walk into Will's office and toss a stack of crisp five-dollar bills on his desk, making a light thud.

I should've asked the bank to give me five hundred one-dollar bills. Lacey's behind Will, pointing at something on the screen. He turns his head, then pulls back.

"What the hell is this?"

"What do you think it is? I lost the bet. There's the money."

"Yes! Yes! Yes!" Lacey cheers, spinning around. "I knew we would win." She scoops the money off the desk and waves the stack in the air. "So who couldn't you resist this time? Not even for a couple of weeks. Do we know her? Is she the bimbo redhead that was here yesterday?"

"Maybe, and I'd appreciate you guys keeping it to yourself. Lacey, no sending text messages to the gang. It's none of their business. This bet was stupid to begin with." She stops counting, and Will leans back in his chair, his forehead wrinkled in confusion.

My phone pings, and I already know it's Daisy. I double-check. Yep. "I'll be right back. She's here."

"Very funny, Josh." Lacey starts counting again. "Seriously? All five-dollar bills."

"Money is money." I chuckle to myself.

I glance at Will. He knows something's up, and he doesn't look happy. We usually tell each other everything. I didn't tell him about seeing Daisy on Monday. He thinks I just went for the meeting and then to Dad's.

"I'll be right back." I turn on my heel, and whispering begins behind my back. Then footsteps patter after me. Lacey and maybe Will.

"You're not kidding, are you?" Lacey mutters, stepping outside. "Shit, it's cold out here."

"Nope. I've never been more serious in my entire life." Daisy and I have been talking nonstop since Tuesday. Something I hadn't thought about before; I think it's good that we haven't seen each other since then. It gives us time to get to know each other and reflect on what happened. I've been counting the seconds until I see her gorgeous face in front of me again, not just on a screen.

I see her, a few feet away, under one of the lamp-posts on the dock, and excitement floods my body. Her face brightens like the sun when she sees me, and she gives me a little wave.

"Whoa. Am I seeing things?" Lacey's voice is thick with disbelief. "You were talking about Daisy?" She yanks on the arm of my jacket. I pull away and walk forward until Daisy is right in front of me.

"Hi, butterfly." She has no time to respond because my lips are on hers in a second, and she melts into me, kissing me just as deeply with her warm lips. How can I be so addicted to a woman in so little time? *Your heart's whispering to you.*

"Oh my gosh, you two are so damn cute. I can't believe it," Lacey gushes behind us, clapping her hands together. "Will, can you believe it? Did we look like that?"

We slowly separate and she wiggles my chin. "Now that's a way to say hello."

"I'd keep doing it, but we have company." I peck her lips one more time, then wrap my arm around her waist, turning in their direction.

Lacey clears her throat. "And you said you were just friends. My ass."

"That was true, but then it just happened." Daisy pushes her body closer to mine.

Will has a slight smile on his face. I think he's even more surprised than Lacey. Maybe that's why he's quiet.

"We'd appreciate it if you'd keep this to your-selves. We'll tell everyone when we feel like it. It's something we have to talk about ourselves. Everyone was hard on our asses last weekend."

"Well, can you blame us? You've never been serious about—"

"Lacey, leave them alone." Will catches her hand and pulls her back. "So what are your plans tonight? Want to catch a quick dinner? It's still early."

Pressure's on. We couldn't wait to be alone all weekend. I rub the back of my neck. "Um. We wanted—"

"Sure. Why not?" Daisy answers. "We're always in a big group, it'd be nice to hang out with you alone and get to know you better. I'm starving."

"Good. Come with me to the office." Lacey pulls her from my arm and they walk off.

Will looks over his shoulder then back at me. "We need to talk," he grimaces. "What the hell is going on? And why haven't you said anything to me?" His voice screams disappointment.

"I don't know. Everything's happening so fast. She's worth way more than any fucking bet."

"And you know this after a week?" he challenges me, propping his hands on his hips.

"Do you hear yourself?" I deflect. "What's with everyone's constant comments? Correct me if I'm wrong, but didn't you fall for Lacey that fast, or was I imagining things?"

"So you're admitting you're in love with her?"

I rake my hands through my hair and start pacing. "No. I don't know. She's all I ever think about, and I physically ache when she's not near me. Just the sound of her voice makes me happy. Whatever it is feels pretty damn good, and I'm not letting her go."

"Yeah, but *we're* leaving in January," he mutters. "Is she aware of that? Do you really want to get seriously involved with someone for the first time in your life, knowing you'll be gone for six months? Daisy isn't someone to throw away after two months. And something tells me she's not going to drop her job like Lacey did either."

I remain silent because I know he's right. He looks at me again and shakes his head.

"Listen, I'm sorry. I want you to be happy, but you've got yourself in a tricky situation. I'd hate to see someone get hurt in the end. Anyway, let's go to dinner." We hug, patting each other on the back.

Maybe I'm the one who'll get hurt in the end.

23

DAISY

I hug Lacey and Will goodbye, then they walk off to their car. During dinner, they promised not to tell anyone about us. I know Will is a little unsure of the situation. His smiles didn't always reach his eyes when Josh and I talked about our... relationship. We don't even know what it is. We just know that we want to be together. Josh doesn't seem bothered by it, though. At least, he didn't have any problem showing me affection in front of them.

Lacey on the other hand was practically jumping out of her seat because she's so happy for us. It drove her nuts when we said not to tell anyone. I'm sure she wanted to call everyone right away. I really don't know why it's such a big deal. Lacey kept crowing about Josh being off the market—how that was something she never thought she'd see. I don't know if I should be happy about that or not.

After I told her I was staying until Sunday, she offered to take the same train as me back to the city. I like it because I'll be able to get to know her better and... maybe I'll divulge my alcohol problem. It wasn't an issue tonight.

As soon as their car is out of sight, Josh wraps his arms around me from behind. I look over my shoulder, and he lowers his mouth to mine. His lips and tongue make me powerless in his arms. It's mind-blowing. What will it be like when we get back to my room? I'm almost nervous because I'm pretty sure I know what will happen.

"Finally, we can be alone. Want to go to your room, or would you rather go out somewhere?"

I twirl in his arms so I'm facing him now. "You couldn't wait to get me alone, and now you're asking if I want to go somewhere else? Let's get in your car and go to my room."

"I don't want to pressure you. Whatever makes you happy, I'll do it."

I push him in the direction of his car. "Drive."

After making out like teenagers in the car, we finally come up for air. I check myself in the mirror and laugh. My lips are red and swollen. "We need to go inside. We have too many layers on," I whisper in his ear with raspy breaths.

He nibbles on my lower lip. "I can't help it that I'm so addicted to you."

"You can nibble all you want upstairs." I pat him on the leg. "Let's go."

"Fine," he huffs, laughing after.

I quietly open the front door. All the lights are on, and there's some chatter coming from the living room. Maybe we can escape upstairs before Patti sees us.

"Daisy!" *Too late.* "Oh, and Josh. How lovely. Funny coincidence, I was just talking to the gentleman in the living room about your marina. Let me introduce you to him." She ushers us through the house. And there go our plans for an escape.

An hour later, we get ready to say our goodbyes. Josh has been glancing at me with fire in his eyes, but I was busy being turned on by his professionalism. The stranger asked some complicated questions about boats and the marina—complicated to me anyway—and Josh had a thorough answer for each one. His knowledge and experience are amazing. He might be a goofball most of the time, but when he's talking business, he means business. Both sides are hot.

Finally handshakes are given and good nights are spoken. With our jackets in hand, we head up the stairs. Patti gave me the same room as last weekend. Once we're at my door, Josh flips me around and cages me in, his chest pulsing against mine.

"If we get interrupted one more time, I'm going to lose my fucking mind." He lowers his head and pulls my shirt to the side, kissing and nipping along my neck. "Open the door, butterfly." I pull the room key out of my pocket and open it. The sly grin on his face right now will never be forgotten.

Once we're in, we drop our jackets and my bag to the floor. Our breathing grows ragged as our hands explore our bodies. I find my back pushed up against one of the posters of the bed. His hands grip my shirt around my waist and tug it free from my jeans. One by one, he loosens the buttons while he ravishes my lips. My chest expands, pushing my breasts against him. He pushes the shirt to my sides and grazes his thumbs across my nipples beneath the lace. I moan into his mouth.

Slowly his hands begin to travel down, but I stop him. His hooded eyes question my reaction. "Just let me quickly go to the bathroom." I kiss him one more time, then step around him. Once I close the door, I brace myself on the sink. Wow, does he know how to kiss. My reflection in the mirror proves it. My hair is already a mess and my lips still plump.

Nerves suddenly crash over me but I beat them down. Even if we don't have sex, I want this. I want him. While I run the water in the sink, I take off my clothes and put on my robe. One last quick glance in the mirror and I open the door.

He sits casually at the edge of the bed with his clothes still on. The comforter has been pulled down and folded at the end of the bed. "I like your robe," he murmurs. His intense stare sends tingles through my body. "What do you have on underneath?" The low, husky tone in his voice soothes me. My nerves subside as I walk closer to him.

"Why don't you find out?" I nudge myself between his legs.

He rests his hands on my hips and wiggles them. "Are you nervous?"

I bite on my lower lip. "A little bit."

"You don't have to be. I want to do this right. I went to the doctor this week and got tested and I'm clean. But you're running the show tonight. You tell me what's okay. I'm in no rush to have sex. We have plenty of time for that. I just want to explore every inch of your gorgeous body and to make you feel good. If you just want me to kiss you and leave, I'll fully understand. I don't want you to do anything that makes you uncomfortable."

And with those words, all my worries and insecurities vanish, and I'm filled with pure trust. I want to make love to him, but I don't think tonight is the night. It's too fast for me.

I cup his cheeks and kiss his tender lips. "Thank you for being so understanding. I'll tell you when I'm ready. But…" I trace my finger along his jawline. "It doesn't mean we can't have any fun."

I step back and untie the belt of my robe, letting it dangle at the sides. His hands reach up and spread the front open, revealing my naked body.

His jaw ticks as his eyes roam my exposed skin. "The secret's out. No tattoos here. Just a couple of leaves on the edges." His warm thumbs trace two tiny ivy leaves on the outsides of my breasts, making me shiver. Then they slowly circle my hardened nipples. "Breathtaking."

I close my eyes as I drown in pleasure. My overwhelming need for him overtakes any rational thought. The robe slides off my shoulders and falls to the ground. I gasp when he pulls me closer and takes one of my nipples into his mouth. Watching him lick and tease them makes me hungry for more.

I reach down and pull his black Henley up over his head and toss it next to my robe. My eyes explore his naked chest as if I've never seen it before. "I could never get sick of looking at you." He guides me backward and stands up, then removes his jeans. He leaves his white boxer briefs on, revealing how hard and aroused he is against the material. My mouth waters and my heart races.

"Tonight, I can look at *and* touch you," he whispers against my skin below my ear. The sensitive part between my legs pulsates just from his words.

I trail kisses along his chest, and goosebumps follow my lips. "I've been waiting days for this moment. Don't make me wait any longer."

He draws me near and sucks one of my nipples deep into his mouth again. My hand grips his hair, encouraging him to keep going. I gasp when he tweaks it with his needy tongue. My legs almost give out. The excitement is almost too much. His strong arm wraps around my waist, holding me up. I arch my back to give his mouth better access.

His other hand brushes over my ass, gripping it and pulling me closer to him. His hardness presses against me and the spark that has been flickering in my chest explodes into a flame, shooting heat all the way to my fingers and toes. I pull away and slide my hand up and down his length. His mouth leaves my skin and a deep moan releases from inside him.

He picks me up and wraps my legs around his

waist, then walks around the bed. I kiss him passionately as he lowers me gently onto the mattress. He hovers over me, his blazing eyes never leaving mine... and then one of his hands slips between my thighs and rubs my entrance, a place no other man has touched before. My breath hitches. The last of my inhibitions are replaced with unleashed desire.

"You like that, don't you? You're so wet."

"Yes. Right there. Don't stop," I pant, almost losing my mind. A seductive smile appears as he slowly slides one finger in, filling me. *Oh my God.* My back arches and I groan when his tongue circles my overly sensitive nipples again. *He's going to be the death of me in the best way possible.* My legs spread wider and I start to pump my hips as he pushes in and out teasingly, a delicious sensation building. "Faster or more. I'm so close."

"I want to feel you. Let yourself go." He slides another finger in and that's all it takes. All control of my body is lost. I grip the sheets with full strength as intense pleasure shoots through my quivering body in warm cascading waves. He captures my mouth when I cry out. My core clenches around his fingers as he prolongs the mind-blowing orgasm.

Slowly the quakes decrease, and he pulls me against his chest. My breathing is ragged, and my muscles feel like jelly. A blanket of pure bliss wraps around me.

Maybe we can do that again and again and again.

24

JOSH

I could watch her like this all day. To listen to her whimpers as I touch her most precious, sensitive spots, making her unravel… it's the most erotic experience. Knowing that no other man has touched her like this makes me want to give her more pleasure and not care about my own.

I pull her against my chest as she comes down from her high. Her breathing slows and she snuggles up against me. "You okay?" I whisper, wrapping my arms around her. She giggles.

"I think you know the answer to that." She kisses my chest, then her mouth closes around my nipple, shocking the hell out of me. She's definitely okay, and I'm standing at full attention. My head falls back onto a pillow and my arms drop to the sides while her hand travels down my stomach to the rim of my briefs. "Let me see what's under here." Her finger slips under the elastic and a delicious shiver overtakes me, imagining her stroking me. "I want to touch you." *Please*. I lift my hips as a hint to pull them off. She gets up on her knees, and I watch, admiring her perfect naked body, as she removes them.

"You just woke up something inside of me that I didn't know existed," she confesses. "So beware. I want to play."

I rest my head on my arm. "Keep doing what you were just doing, and I won't complain. We have all night."

"Do you mean like this?" Her finger brushes lightly up my inner thigh, tickling me, but also sending guilty pleasure straight to my groin.

"Mmhmm. Keep going." I love watching her explore my body with her curious eyes and hands. My breathing increases and sweat covers my skin when her petite hand wraps around me. I push my hips up to encourage her to keep going. "Just like that. My body already loves you." *I love you*. With that one thought, I become even harder and I rest my hand on hers to guide her. To show her what I like.

She leans over me, her pebbled nipples teasing my chest, while we continue to bring me to the edge. Her seductive mouth captures mine. I let go of her hand and cup the back of her neck, pulling her closer, kissing her deeper. My hips move with her hot, slick hand, and I'm on the brink. I pull my lips from hers.

"Dais, I'm going to come."

"Yeah?" She keeps pumping, making my body scream for release.

"It's going to make a mess."

She kisses my neck and whispers in my ear. "I know. I want to see you messy."

Now she's the one covering my mouth with her delicious lips to muffle my moans as I experience the most explosive orgasm I can remember.

Hours later, we lie in each other's arms, tired, hungry, and definitely satisfied. And that's without having sex. Daisy weaves her fingers through mine and squeezes. "This is a night I'll never forget," she whispers. "It wasn't easy to be quiet. I hope I don't get kicked out tomorrow. I made noises I didn't know were possible."

"Maybe they thought you're an opera singer," I say, poking fun at her. She leans up on her side.

"Then we were practicing a duet." I chuckle and pull her closer to me. I'm not sure she could ever be close enough. I'm falling hard and fast, if not already.

"Was it always like this when you were with other women? Well, when you fooled around. Not had sex with?" she asks innocently. I stiffen and lean away from her so I can see her face.

"Daisy. Right now, it's only you and me in this room, and I want to focus on us. On now. To me, my past isn't as important as this moment here with you. I will never compare you to any other woman I've been with because there is no comparison. Tonight was so much more to me because there was emotion involved. I've *never* crossed that line before. I want you and only you. Do you understand that?"

"Yes. I'm sorry." She lays her head on my stomach. "I guess my insecurities sneak out sometimes.

There are no words out there to describe what this night means to me. I was wondering if it means the same to you."

"Butterfly, look at me." She turns over and props herself against a pillow. "Throw your insecurities out the window. You saw and heard what you did to me. That's proof alone about how I feel. You want me to accept your past, and I want you to do the same. If we can't do that, then we'll have a problem."

She sits up, and the sheet falls down, exposing her breasts. My body comes alive *again*.

"I know. I know," she huffs. "I guess I feel like tonight was too good to be true."

"Only good? I thought it was great. No! More like toe-curling spectacular, great."

She throws her head back and laughs, and all the negativity dissipates just by the sound of her giddiness. I find it's a sound I would love to hear every day for the rest of my life.

If someone asked me if I had an addiction, I think I'd say Daisy is becoming mine. Or maybe she already is.

25

DAISY

"Thanks for coming with me into the village," I mention to Lacey. "I didn't get to see as much as I wanted to last weekend. I love the mix of stores and cafés here. And of course, the galleries. It's busy, but more peaceful than the city." I stop and admire our surroundings. There's nothing like the sound of leaves blowing in the wind on a chilly autumn day.

"No problem. Since this is my first fall living in the Hamptons, I've been wanting to explore a little bit too. See some of the changing leaves. The marina is slowing down now that the cool weather has arrived. The guys gave me some time off, so I can take a breather today and tomorrow."

We walk leisurely down the street, window-shopping and chatting. Lacey heads into a cute country-style shop. "Jocelyn asked me to buy a couple of candles for her. We stopped here last weekend, but Pumpkin Spice was sold out. Let's see what they have today." Fifteen minutes later, we walk out with

Pumpkin Spice, Clean Cotton, and Peony Dreams candles. Clean Cotton is for my bathroom.

We get coffees to go from the café next door, then Lacey and I find an empty bench in the sun to enjoy them. Once we're situated, I pull out my phone and check for messages. None from Josh. I shouldn't be so disappointed because he said he had to work on some kind of proposal today. Something that could bring a lot of business to the marina. Oh well.

Yesterday, Josh gave me a tour of the marina and showed me what his day is usually like. Then we took a walk along the beach at sunset. He kept hold of my hand and spoiled me with long, hot, tantalizing kisses that made my fantasies even steamier. We sat on the sand until the orange glow was just a brushstroke in the sky. As soon as we got back to my room, we enjoyed another night-long game of exploring our needy bodies. I'm sure he's memorized all my pleasure points. Watching him lose control because of me is empowering. My cheeks flush just thinking about it.

"I wonder who you're daydreaming about." Lacey taps her coffee cup against mine. "Is that mark on your neck from Josh?"

"What? Where?" I exclaim, feeling my neck, almost dropping my coffee. My heart rate spikes. Lacey bursts out laughing.

"I—" She laughs again. "I was just kidding."

"Phew." I wipe my forehead.

"My ass is killing me from this thing." Lacey readjusts herself on the bench. "Anyway, let's get serious, what were you thinking about?"

"I'm sure you can figure it out. We seem to have similar tastes," I confess, smiling against the rim of my cup. That perks her up. "I'm not talking about the flavor of our coffee either."

"Okay, since you kind of brought it up, now that we're here alone, I want to know how you and Josh got together. I'm not buying it that you were only hanging out as *friends* last weekend. No one else does either." She props one leg up on the bench, then turns toward me with attentive eyes.

"You'll have to buy it. There was only one time when the air shifted and something could've happened, but a wasp stung me, killing the moment. I guess it was a sign."

"But you were already attracted to him, right? I thought I saw a little something when you met at the barbecue in August."

"Hell, yes. The minute I saw him at Jocelyn's house, I was hooked. He's kinda unforgettable."

"I know." She sighs, with a big smile on her face. Beating hearts replace her eyes. "That was me with Will. Those twins sure do make a mark. It's amazing how different they are, though."

"I'm more surprised at how they're identical twins, but I'm only attracted to Josh."

"Well, I'm thankful for that. And call it chemistry." She chuckles.

"I'll be honest, Lacey, I'm a bit scared how strong my feelings are for Josh already. With his track record with women, will he treat me just the same? He swears that what's happening between us is different and that he's never felt this way before. And then the whole St. Thomas thing… being away for six months. I'm almost afraid to get involved. Except I already am."

She purses her lips to the side and nods. "Sometimes you have to take a chance. Love can be painful and messy, but it can also be *so* worth it. I fell for Will fast, if not instantly. I was a fucking mess when I had to fly back home after our vacation. Ask Sky. She had to put me back together. Will and I had just spent a magical night together, and I had to leave early the next morning. I thought I'd never see him again."

As I listen to her, a gust of wind blows past us, and a bright yellow maple leaf attaches itself to my jeans. I pull it off and twirl the stem between my fingers.

Lacey continues with a soft expression on her face. "I thought I'd get over him, and I tried to convince myself that it was just a vacation fling. In the end, Will and I couldn't live without each other. It worked out because I wasn't attached to my job. I was happy to give it up and do what I'm doing now. It's the best decision I've ever made. Josh and Sky worked behind the scenes to get us back together. They were both tired of seeing us moping around."

"A true love story." I sigh. "I'm happy that it worked out for you. Will you always want to go back and forth between St. Thomas and the Hamptons? Do you think you'll get married?"

I'm being nosey because of some of the things Josh said to me on the boat the other day. Are Josh and Lacey thinking what he's thinking, that their living arrangements have to change?

"When we leave in January, it'll be my first time going there for six months. I loved being there on vacation, but I have no idea what it'll be like to actually live there. I can't imagine not seeing my family for six whole months. At least I'll have Will and Josh there."

A stabbing feeling pierces my heart. I drop the leaf onto the bench, and it blows away. Why can't I have fun with him now and not let my emotions take over? *Because you're already in love with him.* I should enjoy the next couple of months, then tell him before he leaves how much my life has changed because of him. Maybe that is the only reason we met to begin with. *Keep lying to yourself.*

Lacey shrugs and keeps talking. "As for marriage, we talk about it but it's not really on the radar yet. We're enjoying being together and him showing me the ropes. If we're in it for the long haul, I need to learn the business and hopefully like it. So far so good. But our living arrangements aren't ideal. Two is company, three's a crowd." She blushes.

"The whipped cream incident?" I crinkle my nose.

"Ugh. That obvious, huh? It was the first time something like that happened. So embarrassing."

"It's getting to be like that with Jules and Sky. I'm wondering if I should switch places with Sky. I could move into her apartment, and she could move into the penthouse. It's just an idea. I haven't mentioned it to either of them."

"Are you crazy? That's not an equal exchange," she protests. "Leaving a penthouse for that tiny, outdated apartment—that's ridiculous."

I swirl the last drop of coffee in my cup. "I don't know. I think I'd like it. To have my own little place to myself. It'd be a welcomed change to finally live on my own. I need to learn how to stand on my own two feet."

Lacey's eyebrows push together. "What do you mean by that?"

"There's more than one reason I live with Julius. There's… something I was going to tell you and the girls tomorrow at lunch, but I can tell you first. Maybe it'll be easier for me."

She grabs my hand. "Gosh, Daisy! What's the matter? Are you sick?"

I giggle. "No, but yes."

She cocks her head. "Not helping."

Just spit it out and get one more thing off your chest.

"I'm a recovering alcoholic. Josh knows already."

She remains quiet, her face revealing nothing. So unlike Lacey. She blinks a couple of times. Awkward silence surrounds us. Then she shakes her head.

"Sorry, I had to process that. I understand now." She pinches her chin. "You've never had alcohol when we're together. I'm so stupid for not putting two and two together. You should've told us sooner."

Time flies by as I answer Lacey's questions, not too unlike the conversation I had with Josh. And just like Josh said, she's supportive, sympathetic, and promises everyone else will be the same.

"Damn, girl! You are a fucking *Powerfrau*!" She practically yells it. I look around quickly to see if there are people nearby.

"A power *what*?"

"Powerfrau… You know… girl power. It's a German word Sophia uses to describe a woman who's kickass. And that is you, my dear. You've been through a lot of shit, and you still ended up on top. You go, girl!"

"Wow. I don't know what to say." Does this family love to make me blush?

"It's true. Never forget it!" She raises her clenched fist in the air, making me laugh.

"My plan was to tell everyone tomorrow at lunch. Now that I've told you, can you do me a big favor so I don't have to repeat this again?"

"Anything you want."

"Can you tell Jocelyn and Christian about it when you're with them tonight? I hate putting that on you, but I want to have fun tomorrow and not have this be the main topic of discussion. As I said, Sky already knows. Oh, Sophia and Drew don't know…." I think about it and shrug. "That's no big deal. They have other things to worry about with the wedding coming up."

"Consider it done. Warning—as soon as Jocelyn sees you tomorrow, she'll hug you until you pop. You're one of us now. We've got your back." *Family.*

"I can totally see it with her. She really knows how

to keep the families together. I admire her for that. She'll be a mess when you leave."

Lacey holds her hand up and looks away from me. "Stop. I can't hear it. I'm already getting emotional about it. So let's get back to you and Josh. Now I understand your worries about a relationship with him. He has gone out with a lot of women, and he drinks when he goes out with his friends. Sometimes he comes home drunk." She cringes. "Sorry. I'm not going to lie about it. But if it makes you happy, that hasn't happened in months... being drunk, I mean."

"It's a lot for both of us to take on," I say. "But we can't think long term yet. He's leaving, and I'm hoping to change a lot of things in my life. And I don't expect him to change anything for me, whether his job or his social life. Well, no. I don't want him screwing around with other girls when he's dating me."

"He wouldn't do that to you. One thing Josh is, is loyal. He never goes out with more than one girl at a time. Granted, the relationships seldom go past one or two dates, but... Ooh, let me share something with you." Her eyes sparkle with secrecy. My eyes widen and I lean in.

"When Josh saw you at the marina on Friday night, I have *never* seen him look at a woman like he did you. Pure excitement, happiness, and adoration. The way he was holding your hand at dinner was freaking adorable. Just him showing affection floored me and Will. And you know what? We loved it. And then Josh brought up their mom. I don't know if I've ever heard him talk about her. He's a changed man.

"Will was even more surprised than me, and maybe a little hurt, because Josh didn't say a word to anyone about you—not even him. You might think it's just fun for him, but with you, this isn't a game. The situation is complicated, but what relationship isn't? He knows you're a keeper, and I'm sure that freaks him the hell out." She grabs my hand and squeezes it. "In a good way."

"So what am I supposed to do? Just wait it out and see what happens?" *And screw around with my heart.*

"I don't know, Daisy. Only you and Josh can decide. Not any of us. Don't listen to the gang joking around and picking on Josh. I know I've been doing it, but he's like another brother to me. We pick on each other. Anyway, on top of being a brilliant businessman and being dedicated to the marinas, Josh is a great guy. If he were just a partier, like most people think, the marinas wouldn't be as successful as they are."

"I wish Julius was here to listen to what you just said."

"From the way I've seen Julius act toward him, it can't be easy at home."

"Yeah." I groan a little. "Wish me luck on that one because I have to deal with him when I get home tonight. He needs to hear it from me that Josh and I are together."

"I love Josh," Lacey says. "He drives me nuts, but he really is one of the good guys. If you've captured his heart, it'll be yours forever. No one can tell you who to like or love. That's your choice. Just don't let it get between your relationship with Julius, though."

"How did you get so experienced? You're better than my therapist."

She glances at her watch. "This'll probably sound like I am a therapist... time's up. We need to get to the train."

I laugh. "Yep, sounds just like her. Hey, thanks for the chat. It was nice to talk to someone who knows Josh so well."

"Anytime. Maybe we'll both end up married to the twins. Then you'll be stuck with me."

What? Married? "I wouldn't complain about that. Let's go."

Maybe it is time to have a chat with Julius. About everything.

"How long have you been working on this?" Will asks as he flips through the financial section of the proposal I've created.

"A couple of months, but most of it just in the last week or so. That's why I've been at the office after hours so much lately."

"I thought it was because you were sick of me and Lacey."

"That too." I chuckle. He throws a heart-shaped stress ball at me that Lacey bought him. "Will, come on. Admit it, it's tight in our place. Something's gotta give. We need to think about our future… as brothers and business partners. I wanted to talk to you alone first because it's always been you and me. Now we're three. You can't tell me you haven't been thinking about your future with Lacey. How does she fit into this scenario? Will you put her name on everything when you get married?" He opens his mouth, but I keep talking.

"Also, the threat of more tropical storms and hurricanes is getting worse. Is it smart to own two marinas? The insurance alone is a killer. And do we really see ourselves ten years from now, still moving back and forth every six months?"

He reclines in his chair and pulls on his lower lip. "It is a lot to think about, and you've made some good points. Do you think Kevin Sanders will go for the idea?"

"My gut says one hundred percent."

"I see you're still cocksure of yourself," he claims.

Speaking of cock… visions of Daisy using her talented tongue to—

"Josh, get your head out of the gutter." He throws something at me but I have no clue what it was. I clear my throat and try to refocus on the plan.

"I think it's a better idea than what Kevin's pushing for, and both sides will win." I put the marked-up draft proposal into a folder and place it to the side. A sense of pride washes over me.

"Since when are you the mature one?" Will looks at me quizzically.

I rest my elbows on my knees and rub my hands through my hair. I lift my head and say, "I've been thinking a lot lately. Or let's say, the last week has confirmed some things." *Daisy.*

Will nods. "I was surprised when you brought up Mom at dinner the other night. It was nice to reminisce. You've never wanted to in the past. You always changed the subject."

"I know, and I regret that. Her death was harder

for me than you think. I internalize my emotions, and you wear them on your sleeve. The weekend I hung out with Daisy when the gang was here, that B&B owner reminded me of Mom."

"Now that I think about it, you're right."

"So many emotions came out, and the memories hit me hard. I opened up to Daisy that day and told her how much I missed Mom. That's the thing with Daisy—it is so easy to be around her. I could tell her anything, and she would understand."

"Ah ha!" He points at me excitedly, and I push back in my chair.

"What the fuck, Will!"

"You're in love with Daisy." He pounds his hand with his fist. "Will you finally admit it? I saw it on Friday when she came to the marina. Your body language practically screamed it, but you refused to admit it. Now I understand the changes in you. Talking about Mom and then this proposal."

"I didn't create this proposal because of Daisy… but it made it easier to finish. I know it's only been a little over a week, but I want to take the chance with her. I can't do that if I'm not here. I don't want either one of us to get emotionally attached if I'm going to leave."

"You didn't deny it, so that means you're already attached. And think about how you were on my ass for weeks when I fell so fast for Lacey. Swearing you'd never fall for someone like—"

"Blah, blah, blah…You've made your point. If you agree with the proposal, with the changes we made, then talk it over with Lacey. I've already pitched it to Joe a little bit since he still owns part of the marina. I'd like Lacey's input as soon as possible. I want to talk to Kevin in the next couple of days."

"I'm in. This better work."

Third ring. She must be busy. We spoke for about two minutes last night. She said she was going to have a big talk with Julius. About what? Let me guess... about us. Or maybe her job situation or even living.

A giant smile greets me on the screen. How does that happy face make my stress disappear? "Hey, sweet thing!" *Huff*. "I'm in Central Park." *Puff*. "I wanted to get a run in before it got dark. Give me a second." From the way her screen is jumping, it looks like she's running in place. Her face glistens from sweat.

"You look hot, all sweaty and panting. But I'd rather you be under me than out there."

She laughs out loud and stops moving. "Don't make me laugh when I already can't breathe. You're lucky I'm already red." She flips her phone around and shows me Central Park, vibrant with color. "Look how beautiful it is here." She flips it back. I'm going to puke from motion sickness. "I wish you were here with me. I feel like I haven't spoken to you in so long."

I chuckle. "We spoke last night, butterfly."

"I know, but it wasn't long enough. We're so damn busy and tired this week."

"So give me the scoop. What did you talk to Julius about?"

"Wait a second, I see an empty bench ahead. It's easier to talk to you when I'm sitting. I hate that we don't live in the same city. I guess it's better than you living in St. Thomas." She sits down, shaking the phone as she does. Large, old trees full of bright red and orange leaves fill the background. She pants and takes a breath. "I had a long talk with him without Sky there. It was important that we were alone."

Tell me about it.

"Anyway, I told him that I'm considering moving out. He thought at first that I was going to say I wanted to move in with you."

Maybe not now, but one day. "I think there could be worse things."

"Exactly. So then I told him the good news about Zane Blue officially signing the contract. And then I told him about us."

"I guess he's going to show up on my front doorstep with a shotgun."

"Don't be crazy. I told him that I know you're leaving in a couple of months, but I want to spend as much time with you as possible until then." She blows me a kiss into the phone. I love seeing her so happy and confident. "He finally accepted our feelings are real and we're happy. And he apologized to me for being such a dick when he found you in our apartment. I told him he needs to apologize to you, not me. I don't need his blessing, but he's going to have to live with my decision."

She takes a large gulp of water from her bottle. "I don't want to regret not having spent enough time with you. So let's take advantage and repeat last weekend again." She wiggles her eyebrows. I hate not being able to kiss her lips. How will I live without them? *Hopefully, I won't.*

"Oh, and I told the girls about my alcohol problems and us too. They were beyond thrilled, which I was surprised about with their previous comments. About us, not the other thing. I don't think they'll be so hard on us anymore. Of course, St. Thomas came up. I can't hear it anymore."

Then why are you bringing it up all the time?

"So you had a good day."

"Yeah, I'm really happy right now. I'd be a lot happier if your cute ass were sitting next to me on this bench or naked in my bed."

"Listen to you."

"I told you, you're a good teacher." She wipes her forehead with her sweatshirt.

"Your imagination and fantasies are all you need." A giggle makes an appearance. "And boy, do I love your fantasies."

"I was at Jocelyn's place, where she designs and sews her dresses. Believe it or not, she gave me a dress to wear to the wedding and a bolero jacket that matches perfectly. Wait until you see it."

"Do I get a hint? How much skin will you be showing?"

"Enough to drive you crazy and then some." *Just*

her talking like this gets me hard. "Other women won't stand a chance."

I cock an eyebrow. "Oh, really. How are you so sure?"

"Because your heart is mine, and I'm not giving it back. And I'll be the lucky one on your arm. At least until January."

Now I'm getting annoyed. "Can we stop talking about me leaving for St. Thomas? I'm not happy that I have to leave either. It's so far away… but you never know how things could change." *Kevin Sanders had better get back to me soon.*

"I'm sorry. I'm just trying to remind myself that this is probably temporary."

"Do you want it to be temporary?"

"Of course not. But I have to face the truth head on. I can't keep thinking that maybe something will keep you here. That's just setting myself up for disappointment. I don't know if I could handle a long-distance relationship, but I would never ask you to change your entire life for me. I know you love what you do."

I love something else too. Time for a change in topic. "Should I pick you up for the wedding? I have to work all day on Friday, but I'll be there early Saturday morning."

"No. I'm helping Julius with pictures before the ceremony starts. The bridal party's getting ready at the hotel, and Sophia wants pictures taken there first. Wait—since you're staying at the hotel, let's go to the church together. I didn't think about that before."

"I'm game. I'm on my own because everyone else is in the bridal party. The most important question is, are you going to stay with me that night? Obviously, I'll have my own room. I think we need to practice our operetta again."

"I hope the walls are thick. I don't know how I'll keep my hands off you all day. And I get to see you in a tuxedo? I'm a dead woman."

"We could always sneak out for a few minutes. No one would ever know."

And maybe, if all goes well, I can tell her my big news.

27

DAISY

The day couldn't be any more beautiful for a wedding. Mid-sixties and not a cloud in the sky. Josh has already checked in, and I'm counting the minutes until I can see him. I have no desire to help Julius with taking pictures. My assistance isn't really needed, but I agreed to do it before Josh and I connected.

Julius and I walk into the hotel and head toward the elevators. "What floor do we need again?" he asks, looking at his watch.

"Fifteenth. Room fifteen-oh-two." I push my small red suitcase into the elevator and glance in the mirror. I don't recognize myself all dressed up like this. Jocelyn was right. This strapless, emerald-green, sequined gown hugs me in all the right places, accentuating my curves, and making me feel like the most beautiful woman in the world. The matching, tapered bolero jacket adds an extra flare to it. And it keeps me warm.

He pushes the button and the door shuts. "What floor is Josh's room?"

"Eleventh."

I watch the button light up for each floor. Eight, nine— Suddenly Julius hits the button for floor eleven.

"What are you doing?" The elevator dings and the doors slide open.

"I know you want to be with Josh. You don't need to be with me. I can handle it on my own."

Something in his eyes says he doesn't mean just for now. In his own way, he's trying to say that we can make it on our own from now on. We're starting new paths in our lives. We'll always be there for each other, but it's time to move on. I stand there with wide eyes. The doors begin to close, but he intercepts them with his arm.

"Go on or I'm going to let them close and you'll be stuck with me."

"Thanks, Jules. I love you." I kiss him on the cheek and rush out of the elevator toward Josh's room. I can hardly contain my excitement.

Of course his room is on the other side of the hotel. I'm winded by the time I knock on the door.

"Daisy?" Josh says from the other side of the door. The door clicks from the inside and then swings open.

My temperature spikes when I see him standing there. The bolero might not be necessary today. Just like the other day when he got out of the shower, a white towel hangs on his gorgeous hips and his hair is in disarray. The difference is, this time he's mine and I can touch him.

His bright green eyes roam up and down my body, making me tingle with need. His towel doesn't hide the way his body is reacting to mine. My eyes lock with his, and that's when I know. I won't give up on us, even when he leaves in January. We'll make it work, even if he's gone for six months. We've captured each other's hearts, and we'll never let go.

"Butterfly," he breathes, love shining in his eyes. "You're stunning. How did I get so lucky?" He grabs my hand and pulls me toward him, embracing me with his protective arms. His mouth ravishes mine before I can respond. Our tongues collide in a sweet madness that takes my breath away and arouses me even more. I wrap my arms around his neck and prolong the kiss, wishing we could stay in this room forever… but we can't.

Our lips part, and he leans his forehead against mine. "I can't help myself when I'm near you. And then you show up looking like a goddess—I've lost all control."

"That was one hell of a kiss. I wouldn't mind if you greeted me like that every time. I'm glad I don't have lipstick on yet. But we need to behave because you have to get ready."

A door closes nearby, and people start talking in the hallway. I giggle.

"Maybe we should close the door," he mumbles. I roll my suitcase in and let the door swing shut. He wraps me in his arms again, kissing my neck. "I've missed you. It's hard going days without holding you in my arms."

"Mmm." I come up for air. "You know how much I love your hugs. I'd gladly stay like this but, again, you need to get ready. I don't want to be late to the church."

He leans his head away. "How come you're here early?"

I place my hands on his warm, bare chest. "Julius knew I was anxious to see you so he practically kicked me out of the elevator when it arrived at your floor."

"I'll have to thank him later." He kisses me gently, then steps back. "Will you help me get into my tuxedo?" He glances at it hanging on the door. "I haven't worn one in a long time."

"I'd rather you be naked, but I'll have to suck it up until tonight."

"Don't use the word *suck* in any sentence today." He traces his finger from the side of my neck all the way down to the swell of my breasts, and goosebumps dance along my skin in its wake. It takes everything in me not to rip the towel off his body. I love that he can do this to me.

I push his hand away playfully. "You're not making this easy. If I have to, I'll wait in the lobby for your gorgeous ass."

His shoulders drop. "Okay. I'll behave."

A few minutes later, I take a step back and bite my lower lip. "Hmm. Not bad for someone who's never tied a bowtie before. Look in the mirror." He slides on his jacket, adjusting it over his shoulders and pulling on the sleeves.

"I'm going to be on the arm of the hottest guy at

this wedding," I compliment him. "Aren't I the luckiest woman?"

He turns around to face the mirror, then kisses my cheek. "And I'm the luckiest man."

"Chop, chop. Time for shoes." He chuckles.

"We'll be on time," he says, sliding his feet into the dress shoes. "By the way, my cousin Vince closed the viewing deck today because of the wedding. Sophia and Drew want to take pictures up there. They're lucky Vince runs the hotel. I don't think any other manager would do something like that."

"Really? I can't wait to see the view." She pushes the tuxedo sleeve up my arm to reveal my watch. "Look at the time. We have to go."

After what feels like an hour, we finally arrive at the church with only fifteen minutes to spare. When we walk through the doors hand in hand, Julius is there checking his camera.

"Hey, Jules. Everything okay?"

He looks up and smiles. Not just at me, but at Josh too. I do a double take. I might pass out. What's happened to make my brother change his mind? Josh and Julius shake hands but don't say anything. I'll process this later.

"Talk to you later, Jules. It's almost time."

Josh and I are ushered to an empty row where we have a good view of the altar. I look around the church and am blown away by how beautiful it is.

"Chloe did a phenomenal job. I don't think I've ever seen this many roses in one place before." Each pew has a mini bouquet of white, pink, and brownish-red roses, hung by a sash of white tulle. Perfect colors to match the iridescent copper of the bridesmaids' dresses and for an autumn wedding. The altar is decorated with four large rose arrangements, placed on tall wooden stands. I'd be afraid they would topple over.

"Look at Drew. I think he's going to pass out," Josh whispers with a chuckle.

I glance at Drew and see him wiping the sweat off his head. Christian mumbles something to him and he smirks.

"All the guys look so handsome. I can't wait to see what Sophia's dress looks like."

Josh intertwines his fingers with mine and rests our hands on my thigh, then leans into me. "Maybe the next wedding will be Will and Lacey's."

"You never know. Or maybe Sky and Jules?"

The organ starts to play, and the bridesmaids make their way down the aisle. Lacey winks at us when she passes. "They all look so beautiful," I gush.

I glance behind us and see Sophia standing at the back with her father. She's wearing a mermaid dress like they said, but not like I imagined. When I thought of mermaid, I expected a big poof at the bottom. With this dress, it hugs Sophia's perfect curves, then the smooth satin flows out toward the floor with a minimal train. The top is a V-neck with a delicate lace and applique bodice. Sheer long sleeves with small patches of matching lace add to the elegance of it.

Her hair is pinned up with a mid-length lace veil. A gorgeous sapphire and diamond necklace adds the final touch. A design from Drew, I'm sure.

Sophia's smile confirms that this is exactly where she's meant to be. I think about how she met Drew and how Lacey met Will. And even Skylar and Julius. They all fell in love instantly. Why should I question how much I'm in love with Josh? It happened when I least expected it, and now my life will never be the same. And I'm so thankful for that.

Sophia passes our row, her eyes glistening as she gazes at Drew at the end of the aisle. Drew wipes a tear from his cheek, and his face reflects all the love he has for her. I find myself doing the same. Josh wraps his arm around me and pulls me close to his side. Right where I belong.

Hours fly by with nonstop eating and dancing. I didn't think I'd have this much fun. I caught Sophia's bouquet, which is so ironic. Of course, everyone had to joke that Josh and I will be the next to get married. I don't think so, but maybe in the future.

"What are you thinking about?" Josh asks, kissing my shoulder. "Does it have to do with us getting naked soon? I know that's what I'm thinking about."

I squeeze his knee. "It's too early. We can't just up and leave."

Will taps Josh's shoulder, then looks at me. "Sorry, can I steal Josh for a second?"

I shrug my shoulders. "Sure."

They walk far enough away that I can't hear them. I pull out a couple of mints and place them on my tongue. Josh will never be able to say I have bad breath. My focus gravitates over to them again. Whatever they're talking about must be serious. Will passes something to Josh, then he pats him on the arm with a grin and walks away. When Josh returns to the table, he puts his jacket on.

"What did Will want? He looked so serious."

Josh bends over and kisses me. "They said we should go upstairs to the viewing deck to take pictures now. Will just gave me the key to get up to that floor. Let's go before everyone else gets up there."

"Good. I could go for some fresh air." I put on my jacket, and we leave the ballroom with my arm looped through his. We step into the elevator where Josh puts the key into a lock next to the floor number. *Twenty-fifth floor*. The door closes, and he gently presses me against the wall, caging me in. Slowly, he kisses along my jawline, making my head spin. I grab his ass and pull him closer.

"Ever make out in an elevator?" I pant in his ear.

He licks my lower lip, then nibbles on it. "Nope. This is my first time."

"That won't be the only first time for something tonight," I respond, teasing him with my fingers along the zipper of his pants. He clenches his jaw to control himself and pulls my hand away.

"No matter how much I want you to touch me, I can't be walking around with a hard-on in front of our friends." I giggle, and then we both straighten our clothes.

"Sophia and Drew look really happy." *I need to*

change the subject. "Her family sure knows how to party and dance. I love that some were wearing lederhosen and those German dresses. I can't remember what they're called. Did you see how your cousin, Vince, was dancing with Sophia's sister, Tessa? There was some definite heat there. Maybe they're the next ones to fall—"

The elevator doors open, and I forget where I am. Josh leads me out the door just before it clips my butt. "Josh, I feel like I'm in a fairy tale. It's so beautiful up here. Look at all these fiery lanterns." There must be at least fifty spread throughout the deck. It's breathtaking and so romantic for pictures. "Did Sophia and Drew request this, or is it always like this up here?" I don't even care about the view of the city.

He leads me through the lanterns and stops in the middle of the deck. "I requested the lanterns for us."

Suddenly my chest feels tight. "What? For us? I don't understand."

His mouth grows into a sweet grin, and he takes my hands in his. "I wanted to do something special for you. To make you smile in that unique way that makes me fall in love with you more every time I see you."

"Wait." I blink several times, then shake my head. *Breathe.* "Did you just say that you love me?"

He pulls me closer and cups my face. "I did, Daisy. I'm in love with you. Is it too early to say this?"

"No," I blurt. My eyes are shiny with tears. "It's not. Because I love you too. I don't care if you have to go to St. Thomas. I know it'll be hard when you're gone, but we'll make it work. We have to."

"I'm not going to St. Thomas."

The air rushes from my lungs, and my hands fall to his hips. "Josh, my heart can't handle that. Tell me it's not a joke."

His lips brush sweetly against mine, and I shudder. "It's not. I promise."

Excitement bubbles in my chest and relief sets in. "Josh——"

He places his fingers on my lips. "Let me finish." I giggle because that's all I know how to do right now. "Before I saw you a couple weeks ago, I had been having discussions about a possible deal with a boat company. The meeting I had last Monday was about this. I wasn't sure which direction to go. But once I found you and I knew my heart belonged to yours, the answer was crystal clear. I'd do anything to stay here with you. Will and I have decided to open a boat dealership at the marina in the Hamptons that I'll run year-round. We're weighing the options on what to do with the marina in St. Thomas. Will and Lacey will go there in January… without me."

"Without you?" I jump into his arms, almost knocking us both over. "I can't believe it. You're really staying! I was praying that something would happen that'd keep you here, but never in my wildest dreams did I think it'd come true."

Our bodies separate, and he gazes into my eyes. "I know everything is going really fast and we still have a lot to learn about each other… and I don't live in the city, but I know in my heart we'll work it out. Everything that has happened in my past has somehow led me straight to you. Once I felt what it's like to truly love someone, I knew I couldn't live without it. You're my world now, and I'm never letting you go."

A tear escapes the corner of my eye. "Nothing matters to me more than us. You see me for who I am, not my past. You know my fears and struggles, and you've seen me at my worst. But you're still by my side. Some days won't be easy, but I believe we'll get through it together. I trust you with my guarded heart and I know I will love you forever."

His lips crash on mine, telling me everything I need to know. It's a kiss filled with love, promises, new beginnings, and no regrets. Clapping and whistles break out around us, making my heart jump out of my chest.

"We're so happy for you," Lacey yells. "Now the gang is complete."

"Hey, I'm still single over here," Chloe chimes in, then laughs. "Doesn't anyone have any single friends anymore?"

"Okay, almost complete. We love you guys," Lacey adds.

"You were in on this together?" I exclaim. "Julius? Even you?" He smiles with a nod. No wonder his attitude changed. I wonder what that story is. Josh squeezes my hand. "And Sophia and Drew? This is your big day. I'm sor—"

"Don't even. This makes it even better. We couldn't be happier," Sophia says with a giant smile.

Drew wraps his arm around her waist and kisses her cheek.

I look around us. Lacey and Will. Skylar and Julius. Sophia and Drew. Jocelyn and Christian. Chloe. My new family and best friends. Who could ask for anything more? Definitely not me.

When we go back to our room, Josh scoops me up into his arms, he looks at me with true love in his eyes. "Daisy, telling you I love you will always be *my* proudest moment."

Maybe this is the end of the series, maybe not. I think I hear more wedding bells in the near future. You'll just have to wait and see. Sign up for my newsletter and follow me on social media for updates.

If you have enjoyed this book, please don't forget to write a review. Thanks!

BOOKS BY KRISTINA BECK

Collide Series

Lives Collide

Dreams Collide

Souls Collide

Collide Series Box Set

Four Seasons Series

Snowflakes and Sapphires – Winter

Passions and Peonies – Spring

Colors and Curves – Summer

Maple Trees and Maybes – Autumn

Standalone Novels

Into Thin Air

Love Ever After Anthology

ACKNOWLEDGMENTS

Wow! I can't believe I just released the last book of the series. Well, maybe... I hinted about possibly writing another book with another wedding, but I have to be careful with my writing schedule. I will keep you posted.

This year has flown by. It feels like yesterday when I released Snowflakes and Sapphires. I truly hope you enjoyed this series and found yourself smiling during this hard time in the world. As COVID has plowed through this year and keeps going, this series wasn't easy to write with all the distractions. However, it did help me lose myself for a little bit and forget about what was going on from day to day. I will miss the characters and the friendships they created along the way.

I have to thank my editor, Rachel Overton, and my proofreader, Helen Pryke, for supporting me during this year. Throwing four books at you in less than twelve months wasn't an easy task on both sides.

But I can't thank you both enough because you really know how to break my books apart and put them back together to make them even better. I've learned so much while working with you both. I'm so thankful that I can count on your thorough work and friendship.

Jody Kaye, where would I have been without you during this series? It was such a pleasure to work with you on this project. You made such gorgeous book covers, I can't express it enough. I truly value our business relationship and most of all our friendship. After the years, we have become close and it's great to be able to support one another as well as bitch about everything. I look forward to working with you in the future.

I have to thank my high school friend, Carlos Castañeda. He was my New York City guru for this series. Whenever I had big or small questions about NYC, he answered right away. I can't thank him enough!

To my beta readers, Rachel and Jamie. You were by my side throughout this series. I know my books are stronger because of you both. Thank you for your support, ideas, and positive feedback.

And to my husband and kids, you always support me no matter what. Whenever I doubt myself, you always do something to boost my morale. Thank you for being by my side, encouraging me to keep going. I love you.

And to my readers, what can I say? You are the best. I've known many of you from the beginning of my writing career. Thank you for supporting my work and spreading the word. It is so thrilling to receive all your wonderful messages about how you have enjoyed my books. I can't wait to write more for you.

Stay safe and healthy during these trying times. We will get through it together. Let's try to stay positive and hope 2021 is a better year for all of us.

ABOUT THE AUTHOR

Kristina Beck was born and raised in New Jersey, USA, and lived there for thirty years. She later moved to Germany where she lives with her German husband and three children. She is an avid reader of many genres, but romance always takes precedence. She loves coffee, dark chocolate, power naps, flowers, and eighties movies. Her hobbies include writing, reading, fitness, and forever trying to improve her German-language skills.

For more updates on her books, sign up for her newsletter and follow her on social media. www.kristinabeck.com

facebook.com/krissybeck73

instagram.com/krissybeck96

amazon.com/author/kristinabeck

bookbub.com/authors/kristina-beck

goodreads.com/kristina_beck

Printed in Great Britain
by Amazon